"I don't know anything about *Englischer* children..."

Thomas smiled sadly. "Me neither."

"We'll figure it out," Patience said.

"I'd hoped to make a Plain girl of her faster than this," he admitted ruefully. "But God teaches patience with children. Isn't that what they say?"

"It is." She smiled. "And I'm about to have a whole schoolhouse full of them, so maybe you should feel grateful for just one."

Thomas cracked a smile then, and laughed softly. "Maybe I should." He jutted his chin toward the door. "I'm going to go hitch up the buggy."

Patience watched as he headed out the side door, and she put a hand over her pattering heart. She wasn't blind to his broad shoulders and warm smile—it would be easier if she were, because it wasn't that she didn't want to marry...she did. But she was going to be a disappointment to whoever tried to court her.

Patience was a teacher and a helpful neighbor. Nothing else. She'd best remember it. Strong hands and broad shoulders didn't change that she wasn't the wife for Thomas.

Patricia Johns writes from Alberta, Canada. She has her Hon. BA in English literature and currently writes for Harlequin's Love Inspired and Heartwarming lines. You can find her at patriciajohnsromance.com.

Books by Patricia Johns

Love Inspired

Redemption's Amish Legacies

The Nanny's Amish Family

Montana Twins

Her Cowboy's Twin Blessings
Her Twins' Cowboy Dad
A Rancher to Remember

Comfort Creek Lawmen

Deputy Daddy
The Lawman's Runaway Bride
The Deputy's Unexpected Family

Harlequin Heartwarming

The Second Chance Club

Their Mountain Reunion

Home to Eagle's Rest

Her Lawman Protector
Falling for the Cowboy Dad
The Lawman's Baby

Visit the Author Profile page at Harlequin.com for more titles.

The Nanny's Amish Family

Patricia Johns

LOVE INSPIRED
INSPIRATIONAL ROMANCE

Recycling programs
for this product may
not exist in your area.

LOVE INSPIRED®
INSPIRATIONAL ROMANCE

ISBN-13: 978-1-335-48818-3

The Nanny's Amish Family

Copyright © 2020 by Patricia Johns

This edition published by arrangement with Harlequin Books S.A.

For questions and comments about the quality of this book, please contact us at CustomerService@Harlequin.com.

Love Inspired
22 Adelaide St. West, 40th Floor
Toronto, Ontario M5H 4E3, Canada
www.Harlequin.com

Printed in U.S.A.

A father of the fatherless…
God setteth the solitary in families.
—*Psalm* 68:5–6

To my husband—
you're the best choice I ever made! I love you.

Chapter One

Thomas Wiebe pushed himself to his feet and headed toward the side door to look out at the warm August evening. Low, golden sunlight washed over the grass, and birds twittered their evening songs. His jittery nerves didn't match the peaceful scene. The social services agent who had come by the night before had said that they'd be here by seven, and it was a quarter past already.

"Stop fussing, Thomas," Mammi said, pulling a boiling kettle from the woodstove. Her crisp, white *kapp* was a shade brighter than her white hair. "She'll come."

Thomas glanced back at his family in the kitchen. They weren't all blood relatives, but this was as close to family as he had left in the community of Redemption, Pennsylvania. His older brother, Noah, sat with a glass of lemonade in front of him, his straw hat on the table. Thomas and Noah were both old enough to be married with families of their own by now, but not having found the right wife meant that they stayed here with Uncle Amos—an honorary uncle, not a biological one—and his elderly grandmother. It was a house filled with men, as Mammi described it.

And any minute now, Thomas's daughter would be joining them… *His daughter.* He'd known about her, but he'd never been given the option to be in her life. Thomas had made a mistake with an Englisher girl on his lengthy Rumspringa, and the breakup had been messy. Tina wanted nothing more to do with him. It wasn't that he forgot about his daughter, but he'd accepted that heartbreak as part of the consequences for his mistakes. Coming back home to Redemption four years ago was supposed to be his new start. But when a social services agent came to his house last night and told him of a fatal car accident that killed his daughter's mother, everything had changed.

His daughter, Rue, was now coming to live with him after never having met him even once in her young life. Would she hate him just a little? He wouldn't blame her. But at the age of four, he wasn't sure how much she'd even understand about her new situation.

Outside, a car rumbled up the drive, and Thomas pulled open the screen door and stepped out onto the raised patio next to the house. A clothesline full of men's pants and shirts flapped in a warm breeze.

Thomas waited while the car stopped, the door opened and the social services agent from yesterday got out. She shot Thomas a smile and waved. She was an older woman, plump and pleasant. Tanya Davis, she'd said.

"Good evening, Mr. Wiebe!" Tanya called.

Thomas would do just fine, but he didn't trust himself to speak just yet. He came down the steps toward the car and glanced back to see Noah and Amos in the door. Tanya opened the back door to the car and leaned in, undoing the buckles from a children's car seat. Then she backed out again, followed by a small, frail child.

The little girl stood there, a teddy bear clutched in front of her. She wore a pair of pink pants and a ruffled purple T-shirt. Her hair was stringy and blond, and she looked around herself with large, frightened blue eyes. She reminded him of a bedraggled bird.

Thomas came closer, unsure if he'd scare her or not.

"Hello," he said in English. He wasn't very eloquent in English... But then he wasn't very eloquent in German, either.

The little girl looked at him, silent.

"I'm your *daet*, it would seem," he said slowly. Then he realized she might not know the word. "I'm your... father."

"Hello, Mr. Wiebe." Tanya held out a hand and Thomas shook it. "Shall we go inside? Maybe you're hungry, Rue," Tanya said quietly, smiling down at the girl, then glancing up at Thomas.

"Yes, Mammi has made some sticky buns. She thought you might like that," Thomas said.

He turned around and led the way to the house, feeling that strange distance between himself and that little girl behind him. Rue had never met him, but he'd also never had a chance to even see her... He'd been a *daet*, but until this very moment, it had been theoretical. How was he supposed to do this—be a *daet* to an Englisher child? There was a time he thought he could be an Englisher himself, but that was when he was young and foolish, and he'd forgotten that it wasn't possible to change what a man was born to.

Tanya brought Rue indoors, and introductions were made. Amos. Noah. Mammi. Mammi's name was Mary Lapp, but she was never called Mary in this house. Rue stared silently around the room, looking stricken. Thomas sank down to his haunches in front of her.

"Hello, Rue," he said quietly.

"Hello…" she whispered.

"This is all very new, isn't it?" he said.

"Yes. I want my mommy…" Tears welled in her eyes, and Thomas reached out and patted her shoulder.

"Have you had a…daddy…before?" He hesitated over the English word. Had Tina moved on with another Englisher man? That was what he was asking.

"No, never," she whispered. His heart clenched. How much wrong had he done in that woman's life? He'd known better, and he wouldn't ever completely forgive himself for the way he'd conducted himself in that relationship.

"You'll call me Daet," he said softly. "And I'll take care of you. You'll be safe and happy here, *yah*?"

Rue wiped her eyes on her teddy bear and looked hesitantly around the kitchen again. Her bright pants and T-shirt were in stark contrast to their plain clothing.

"Where's the TV?" Rue whispered.

"We don't have a TV," he said.

"How come?" She frowned, peering past him as if

he were hiding it somewhere, and Thomas couldn't help but smile.

"Because we're Amish, Rue. You'll get used to our ways."

It didn't seem to be the right thing to say because Rue's eyes filled with tears again, and he looked helplessly toward Amos and Noah. He wasn't quite so comforting for the little girl as he'd hoped, and he didn't know how to cross that divide.

"Thomas, pick her up," Mammi said, waving a hand at him. "She's just a tired little thing, and she needs to be held."

Thomas looked hesitantly around, and when Tanya nodded her approval of the idea, he gently picked Rue up and rose to his feet. She was light and small in his arms, and when he gathered her close, she leaned her little head against his shoulder and exhaled a shaky sigh. It was then that he felt it—that wave of protective love.

"All right, then," he murmured. "All right, then."

"Are you all set up for Rue to stay?" Tanya asked.

"Yes, she'll sleep in a little bed in Mammi's bedroom," Amos said, speaking up. "Mammi—" He hesitated. "That is, Grandma to us. So the child won't be alone."

"I'll take care of her with the washing and dressing and such," Mammi said. "She'll be well cared for."

"And we have another young woman coming to help," Amos added. "She'll arrive in a few minutes to meet Rue."

"It sounds like you're prepared, then," Tanya said. "I'll go get Rue's suitcase from the trunk."

The older woman disappeared out the door, the screen clattering back with a bang.

"So, the new schoolteacher said she'd help?" Thomas asked, shooting Uncle Amos a questioning look.

"She did," Amos replied. "I'm sorry, I meant to tell you. She's a nice young woman, too. You should take note—with a child, it's high time you get a wife."

As if Thomas could even think about courting right now. He looked down into Rue's pale little face. The delicate skin under her eyes looked almost bruised from lack of sleep, and he reached up and brushed her hair away from her forehead. He was still taking her in, looking her over, trying to see himself in that little face. He could see her mother there—the hair, the eyes. Was he there, too? He must be, but it was hard to tell.

There was a tap on the door and Amos went to push open the screen. Thomas looked up, expecting to see the social services woman again, but this time a young Amish woman stepped inside. She wore a purple dress, and her apron was gleaming white. Her hair was golden—the part he could see before it disappeared under her *kapp*—and she smiled hesitantly, looking around the kitchen.

"This is Patience Flaud," Amos said. "She'll be teaching school here starting in September, and she's staying with the Kauffmans."

Hannah and Samuel Kauffman lived on the next acreage over, and Hannah and Mammi were good friends—they had coffee together at least twice a week and they'd been known to help each other out with canning and washing days.

Patience, however, was distinctly younger than old Hannah Kauffman…and prettier. Thomas swallowed.

"You asked me to help out?" Patience said.

"Yah," Thomas said, stepping forward with his daughter in his arms. "We haven't met yet. I'm Thomas Wiebe, and this is my daughter, Rue."

Patience smiled at the girl, cocking her head to one side. "Ruth, is it?" she asked in German.

"No, Rue. She's Englisher." As if her clothing wasn't glaring enough. Thomas felt heat flood his face. "It's… a long story. She doesn't know German. But she's mine, and I'll need a woman's help."

"Besides me, of course," Mammi said. "I'm not as young as I used to be, and I'm not sure I could chase down *kinner* if the need arose. Safety, you know."

"Rue, then," Patience said, switching to English, and her gaze flickered up to Thomas, sharpening slightly. She'd have questions, no doubt. Everyone would, and his reputation as a good, Amish man looking for a wife was officially tarnished. He'd now be the Amish man with an Englisher child looking for a wife—very different.

"Hello, Rue. I'm Patience," she said softly and she glanced over to the table where the older woman had set down a pan of cinnamon buns. "Are you hungry? Mammi has some sticky buns."

Rue lifted her head from Thomas's shoulder and looked toward the table.

"Have you ever had a grandmother before?" Patience asked.

Rue shook her head.

"Well, you have one now. This is Mammi. *Mammies*

are kind and sweet and they cook the best food…" Patience bent down conspiratorially. "I'm glad to meet your new *mammi*, too!"

Mammi smiled. "Come now, Rue," she said gently. "I think you'll like my sticky buns."

Thomas put Rue back down and she went toward the table, sidling up next to Mammi like a hurt animal looking for protection. Mammi bent down to talk to her, and Thomas heaved a sigh.

"She looks very sweet," Patience said, and Thomas glanced over. Patience met his gaze with her clear blue eyes, and for a moment, he felt all the words clam up inside him. Why did the schoolteacher have to be so distractingly pretty?

"Yah," he said after a moment. "I've just met her, myself."

"How did that—" Patience stopped and blushed. "I mean, this is the first you've met her?"

"I had a rebellious Rumspringa," he said quietly. "One I learned from. I'm not proud of that."

In fact, he'd meant to keep the secret for the rest of his days, if he could. What use was it to the community to advertise his weakness? But that secret was no longer possible, and his mistakes were about to be very public.

"I'm not judging," she murmured.

But she was. Everyone would. Thomas would, too, if he were in their place. What did she think of him *now*?

The door opened again, and the social services woman came inside with a suitcase, and things turned official once more. There was discussion of dental visits, doctor's appointments and counseling for the family to help with the transition if they should feel the need.

"No," Thomas said, shaking his head. "We have our ways, and if there is one thing our people do, it's raise *kinner*. She'll be loved…dearly."

Emotion choked off his voice, and he forced a smile as he shook Tanya's hand in farewell.

"Congratulations, Mr. Wiebe," Tanya said. "You have a beautiful daughter."

"Thank you," he said.

That was the first anyone had congratulated him yet. Noah, Amos and Mammi had reassured him, but that was a different sentiment. In this community, Rue was a shock. Not only did Thomas have to confess to a rather large mistake in her conception, but he was bringing an Englisher child into their midst. The Amish understood the trouble he'd brought to everyone, and one did not congratulate a mess.

"I'm going to give you my phone number, and some information to help you in this transition," Tanya went on, and for the next few minutes, he attempted to grasp all that she was saying. The Englishers had their ways, but the Amish would pull together and deal with this the way they always had—with community. He accepted the pamphlets and brochures that she handed to him before walking out the door.

There were always consequences—to his own household and to the community. The Amish protected their boundaries for a reason—there were other young people who could be influenced. Their way of life was not only an act of worship, it was a wall between themselves and the world. He'd just brought a piece of the outside world into their midst in the form of his tiny daughter. There would be strong opinions, he had no doubt, and he couldn't blame his neighbors if they voiced them.

This was precisely why a man needed to behave himself before marriage, and now he must shoulder those consequences. Thomas stood there by the door for a moment as he listened to the social services agent start her car.

Gott, guide me, he prayed silently. *I know I went wrong out there in the world, but she's just a little mite, and... She's mine.*

He was Rue's *daet*. Nothing would ever be the same again.

Patience went into the kitchen and opened a cupboard, looking for the plates. Mammi stood at the table, slicing the cinnamon buns apart with a paring knife, but she'd need plates to serve them on. This was Patience's role in any Amish home—to help out in the kitchen. She didn't need to be asked, and she didn't need permission. She found the plates in the second cupboard that she checked, and she glanced over at the table to do a quick head count.

Thomas stood beside the table, and his gaze was trained on her. He was a good-looking man—tall with broad shoulders and dark eyes that could lock her down... But he didn't seem to see her, exactly. He seemed more to be deep in thought. And could she blame him? His life had just turned upside down.

Patience brought the plates to the table, and Mammi

used the tip of the knife to pry up a cinnamon bun and plop it onto a plate. When she gave the first plate to Amos, he slid the cinnamon bun in front of Rue instead, and a smile lit up the girl's face.

The men were served first, so she accepted a cinnamon bun from Mammi and angled her steps around the table and over to where Thomas stood.

"For you," she said, holding out the plate.

"No, no…" Thomas shook his head. "You eat it."

Patience held the plate but didn't take a bite. "Are you all right, Thomas?"

He roused himself then. "*Yah.* I'm fine."

She followed his gaze to the little girl. Rue looked so out of place in her Englisher clothes. Pink and purple. And pants on a girl, too—it wasn't right. But all the same, Rue was such a slender little thing—her head looking almost too big for her body.

"She needs some dresses," Patience said.

"*Yah.*" Thomas brightened. "The social services woman left all these Englisher clothes, but when we get her some proper Amish dresses, it will be better, won't it?"

"Yes," Patience said with confidence she didn't exactly feel. "I think so, at least."

Thomas relaxed a little. "Amos said you'd agreed to help us."

"It's no problem," she said. "For a week or two, at least."

Thomas nodded. "I'm grateful. This was a pretty big shock for me, so I'm not ready for…any of it."

"Understandable," she said.

"Would you be willing to do some sewing?" he asked, lowering his voice. "Because Mammi doesn't see as well as she used to—"

"I can sort out some girls' dresses," she replied with a small smile. "They're quick enough to sew."

"Rue doesn't know our ways, at all," Thomas said. "Rue's life, up until now, has been entirely English. I'm not even sure that her *mamm* told her who I was. Tina—Rue's *mamm*—didn't want me in her life, and I didn't have a whole lot of choice. I was coming home to rededicate my life to our faith, and Tina hated me."

So he *had* known of his daughter…

"Why did she hate you?" Patience asked, then she felt the heat hit her cheeks. This wasn't even remotely her business.

"Because I wanted to go home, and I didn't want the life she did." Thomas looked away, pressing his lips together. He'd probably already told her more than he wanted to.

She had so many questions, but none of them were appropriate to pose. She'd been asked to come help, not to put her nose into another family's affairs.

"How can I help?" Patience asked quietly.

"I need my daughter to learn to be plain," he said. "And the sooner the better. I'll show her what I can, but she needs a woman to show her how an Amish woman acts. Mammi is getting old, and she can't chase down a four-year-old if she decides to bolt. I need Rue to know how to be one of us."

"That's a lot to ask," Patience said softly.

"I know. You're not here for this. You're here to teach school—" he began.

"No, I mean, it's a lot to ask of *her*," Patience said with a shake of her head. "She's very young, and only just lost her mother. We're all strangers to her, and she doesn't even speak our language. Teaching her to be Amish might be too much to ask of her. Right away, at least."

"What are you suggesting, then?" Thomas asked.

"That we just teach her that she's loved," Patience said. "The rest will come with time."

Thomas met her gaze, and his shoulders relaxed.

"Is that enough, do you think?" he asked.

"For now, yes." For as much as her opinion counted in this.

"And you would know *kinner*, wouldn't you?" he said. "How long have you been teaching?"

Patience dropped her gaze, suddenly uncomfortable. "This will be my first position. I might not be much of an expert."

"Oh…" Thomas eyed her a little closer.

"I love *kinner*, though, and I really needed a fresh start."

"Why?"

It was a loaded question, because everyone knew that a girl didn't grow up longing to teach school. She grew up planning for her own husband and houseful of children. A girl didn't plan her life around a job—she planned her days around a home. And at twenty-three, Patience was very nearly an old maid. But she'd asked a few probing questions of her own, so she supposed she owed him an answer.

"There was a proposal," she admitted. "That I could not accept, and… It was better to come away, I thought."

"Oh…" He nodded. "I'm sorry."

Mammi approached with another plate, and Patience stepped back to allow the older woman to press the plate into Thomas's hands.

"Eat now," Mammi said, patting his arm gently. "It is what it is, Thomas. You still need to eat."

It was the same thing that Patience's mother had said when Patience had turned down Ruben Miller's proposal. Ruben's proposal had seemed quite ideal—he was widowed with five children of his own, all under the age of thirteen. And if Patience could be his wife, she could help him raise his *kinner*—a ready-made family. But when Ruben proposed, he'd spoken rather eloquently about the future babies they'd have together.

"Does it matter so much?" Patience had asked. "If you have five children already, do more babies mean so very much to you?"

"Babies are blessings!" he'd said. "Patience, what is a marriage without *kinner* to bind you? You'll see—you'll want to have *kinner* of your own. And the *kinner* will want babies to play with, too. You're young. We could have another seven or eight before we're done."

Ruben had said it all with such a smile on his face that any other girl would have been swept off her feet in anticipation of all those babies, the children to raise, the family to grow. Patience's secret had been on the tip of her tongue, ready to reveal why the babies were a worry for her…

And she didn't tell him. She *should* have told him, perhaps. But she didn't.

"Eat," Mammi said, turning her attention to Patience, and the old woman tapped her plate meaningfully.

Patience peeled a piece of cinnamon bun and popped it into her mouth. Mammi was right, as was Patience's own mother. No matter what came a person's way, they were obligated to eat and keep up their strength. Because there was still work to be done—always more work.

"It will be better, Thomas," Mammi said, lowering her voice, even though she was speaking in German and Rue wouldn't understand. "When you marry and have more children, she'll be one of many. More children will nail her down properly. You'll see."

More children—yes, that was very likely the solution for Thomas Wiebe. If he got a good Amish wife and had more children, then Rue would grow up in a proper Amish household. She'd be an older sister. Responsibilities helped a child to feel like they belonged.

Hadn't that been Ruben's solution to any marital difficulties? And he wasn't alone. Amish people wanted children. Their lives and their faith revolved around the home. Even the rules of the Ordnung were set in place to keep families close together. Parents and children were the center of their lives.

Patience turned away from Thomas and Mammi, who continued to talk together, their voices low. She took another bite of the buttery, sweet cinnamon bun.

She should have told Ruben the truth when he proposed—told him that she could not have any children of her own—because marrying a man who needed a *mamm* for his children was the perfect solution, if that man could be happy with no more babies. If she'd told Ruben the truth about the surgery to remove the tumors and how it left her infertile, would he have still married her? Patience hadn't been sure, and when faced with the older man's hopeful gaze, the words had died on her tongue.

Patience would never be a *mamm* to her own children. She'd never be pregnant or have babies. And she'd wanted nothing besides a family of her own since she was a girl. So she was grieving all that she was losing, too, and she hadn't had the strength to walk Ruben through it all. That surgery to remove the tumors might have saved her life, but it had ended any chance she had at living the life she longed for.

But work helped her not to think too much about the things she could not change, and teaching was supposed to provide that distraction for her. Until the teaching started, she could distract herself with this little Englisher child—there would be work enough to go around.

"Tomorrow, if you could find me some fabric, I could start making a dress or two for Rue," Patience said, turning back.

"Our carpentry shop is right next door to the fabric store," Thomas said. "I'll bring you with us to work in the morning, and you can choose whatever you need. Then I'll drive you both back."

"Thank you. That would work well." She glanced back at the men at the table, the old woman seated next to Rue, already coaxing a few smiles out of her. "Unless you need me for anything more, I could let you and your family have some privacy."

Sewing some little dresses would not be difficult, and it would be good for the girl to wear some looser, more comfortable clothing. And it would also be good for Patience to keep her fingers busy. Work made the hours pass by and brought meaning to the daylight hours.

It was the evening that she dreaded, when the work was done and she crawled alone into her bed at night. It was then that she faced all the things she longed for but would never have.

Like children of her own.

Chapter Two

Thomas stepped outside, holding the screen door open as Patience passed through. He pulled it shut behind him, giving a thin screen between him and the others—it was something. Closing the door outright wouldn't have been appropriate. They were both single, after all.

Thomas rubbed his hands down the sides of his pants, still feeling a little uncomfortable around this woman. The sun was sinking below the horizon, washing her complexion in a rosy pink, and Thomas did his best not to act like it mattered to him. He wasn't some young man looking to take a girl home from singing—he was a *daet* now. And a mildly confused *daet*, at that.

Thomas glanced over his shoulder toward the back yard; a white chicken coop sat next to the fence. The chickens had all gone back into it for the night, the cock standing outside, surveying the bare dirt surrounding the structure like a guard. The rooster crowed hoarsely.

"If you could come back in the morning, that would be really helpful," he said.

"I'll see you in the morning, then," Patience said, and as she looked up at him, he realized that her blue eyes were fringed with dark lashes. An odd detail to notice, but one that he liked.

"*Yah*. I'll see you then," he said with a quick nod. "Thank you. I appreciate you helping us."

She shrugged. "We help where we can."

"I'd like to pay you back somehow—"

"That isn't necessary," she said. "I was here, and I was able. That's enough."

And maybe she was right. The Amish helped each other in times of need—it was what bound them together. But she was new here, and she already had a classroom waiting for her. To take this preparatory time and use it with his daughter was a sacrifice that he appreciated.

"I'm a carpenter," he said hesitantly. "I could help you, too. You should come by my shop. Maybe there is a piece of furniture, or—"

"I'd have nowhere to put it," she said. "I'm a single woman teaching school. I have no home of my own."

"Not yet," he said with a wry smile. Did she have no idea how lovely she was? There would be men lining up in Redemption for a chance with her. And perhaps that was why she came to a new community—for new marriage options. "When you marry, you can count on me to make you a cabinet."

"You're very kind." Her expression saddened and she dropped her gaze. Of course—he'd already forgotten about that man who had proposed… Maybe she'd loved him, and her reasons for turning him down had gone deeper.

"I'm sorry," he said awkwardly. "I'd forgotten about... the proposal."

"Life moves on," she said.

"Why did you say no?" he asked. "If I can ask that."

"Because I wouldn't have made him happy," she said, shrugging.

"He must have disagreed with that," Thomas said. She wasn't seeing herself through a man's eyes, obviously.

"He didn't know everything," she said. "And I know myself better. I wouldn't have been the wife he wanted."

Patience knew her mind, and she'd been willing to not only turn down an offer, but move to a different community. Thomas could only respect that she knew what she was talking about. Not every woman had such high character. Uncle Amos's wife ran away after less than a year of marriage, dooming Amos to a life of solitude, and Thomas had seen firsthand how lonely that had been for the older man. At nearly forty, Amos should have a houseful of *kinner*. There could be no remarriage for an Amish man. Those vows were for life. So if Patience had chosen the harder path, it was likely the right path to take.

"He might thank you later, then," Thomas said.

"I hope so," she replied. "He's a good man, and another woman will be happy to snap him up."

Yes, there would be women less beautiful than Patience waiting for a chance. And he looked at her quizzically. She wasn't what he expected.

"I'm grateful you're here to help me with my daughter," he said. "All the same."

Patience took a step down the stairs, then looked back at him over her shoulder. "It will all work out for good, Thomas."

Was she talking about her situation, or his? Yes, that was what their faith told them, that all things worked together for good for those who loved Gott. But sometimes the working out took some time to get to. Hearts broke... And while Gott brought comfort, it wasn't immediate. It was more like spring growth.

"Good night, Patience," he said.

Patience smiled, and then turned and continued walking up the drive. His gaze lingered on her retreating figure for a couple of beats, and then he turned and pulled open the screen door once more. He went inside, past the washing-up sink in the mudroom and into the kitchen.

Noah stood with his hands in his pockets and he met Thomas's gaze with a helpless look of his own.

"She'll be back in the morning," Thomas said. It would be a big help.

"*Yah*, that's good." Noah looked toward the kitchen sink. "I'll do the dishes."

The older Mammi got, the more like bachelors they all lived—cleaning up after themselves. Mammi was elderly, and she couldn't do it alone.

"No, no," Mammi said, as she always did. "That's women's work."

"That child needs a woman tonight, Mammi," Noah replied. "I can wash up the dishes."

Rue sat at the table next to Amos, a half-finished cinnamon bun in front of her. Her eyes were drooping, and her little shoulders sagged as if under a heavy burden.

"I've got a nightgown for her," Mammi said. "It's a bit big. Looking at her, I could probably wrap her in it twice."

"We might need to let her wear her own clothes," Thomas said, looking toward the suitcase in the corner. "Until we can sort out something more appropriate."

"Yah..." Mammi said with a sigh. "We might need to."

He could hear the regret in her voice—those Englisher clothes were jarringly different from their Amish garb, and for him they were a reminder of those years he'd spent away from their community.

"I'll carry the suitcase upstairs for you, Mammi," Amos said, rising to his feet.

Rue looked up as Amos stood, then she turned tear-filled eyes onto Thomas. "I want my mommy."

Thomas sank down on his haunches next to her. "I know, Rue."

"But she's dead," she whispered.

"Yes..." Thomas felt his throat thicken with emotion. "Did your mommy tell you about Heaven?"

"Yes..." Rue's chin trembled.

"Then you know that God is taking care of you," Thomas said quietly. "And He's taking care of her, too."

The girl looked at him in silence. Did it mean anything to her right now? He wasn't even sure. She was very young, and he didn't know how much faith Tina had raised her with. Tina hadn't been a strong believer when he'd known her... And he hadn't been much of an example of a Christian man's behavior, either. That was something he wouldn't forgive himself for, and a mistake he'd never make again. He'd keep himself under control, and he'd find an appropriately Amish wife.

"It is time for bed now," Thomas said.

"No."

Thomas looked down at her, uncertain if he'd heard the girl right. "Come, Rue. Mammi will help you get your pajamas and she'll show you your bed."

"No." Rue hadn't raised her voice, but she did tip her chin up just a little bit.

Amish children didn't say no at bedtime. At least he didn't think so. He didn't have any other children to compare this with, and he looked over at Mammi uncertainly.

"Come, Rue," Mammi said, smiling. "We'll get you dressed for bed."

"No!" Rue shook her head and leaned back into the chair. "I don't want to!"

Mammi's eyes widened, and Noah laughed softly from where he stood at the kitchen sink, filling it with sudsy water.

"You don't want to go to bed," Thomas said.

"I don't want to."

"What if…" Thomas rose to his feet and rubbed a hand over his rough chin. "What if you got your pajamas on, then you came back downstairs and I told you a story?"

Rue eyed him uncertainly. "I want TV."

"But without a TV, a story might be nice," he said,

raising an eyebrow. "Don't you think? I know all sorts of good ones."

Mammi made a disapproving sound in the back of her throat, and Thomas realized he was likely digging himself into a hole with this little girl, but she couldn't be blamed for not knowing their ways, or even for resenting them just a little bit. She'd lost her mother, after all. What was the harm in a story or two to put her to sleep on this first night in a strange home with no TV?

"She must learn to obey," Mammi said in German.

"But first she must learn to like it here," Thomas replied, then a smile tickled at his lips. "And we have no TV. That is a serious problem for an Englisher child."

Mammi wasn't amused, but Thomas was the *daet*, so she held out her hand to Rue.

"Come, Rue," she said in English. "You'll get your pajamas on, and then come back down to your *daet*. Okay?"

Rue slid off her chair, casting a tiny little smile in Thomas's direction before she took Mammi's hand and followed her up the staircase.

Noah stood at the sink washing the dishes, the water turning on for a moment as he rinsed a plate and put it in the dish rack.

"Am I wrong?" Thomas asked.

"What do I know?" Noah said with a shrug. "I'm not a *daet*."

And up until yesterday when he'd heard that his daughter was coming home to him, he hadn't felt like one, either. But he'd have to catch up, and he'd have to teach Rue their ways. He was just grateful for the family surrounding him that would help him in this new role of father.

"I should tell you, Noah. I talked to our *mamm* yesterday," Thomas said, and his brother turned to look at him, his gaze suddenly guarded.

"When?" Noah asked.

"At the government office. She was the one who helped them find me."

Their mother, Rachel Wiebe, had looked so different dressed in a sleeveless Englisher dress and wearing a few pieces of jewelry. Her hair was dyed—the gray that had started to creep into it was now gone. She didn't look like a *mamm*. She looked… English.

"How is she?" Noah asked.

"She's healthy and happy." He'd wanted to see her miserable—realizing her mistake. But that hadn't been the case. "She wants to get to know Rue."

Noah sighed and turned back to the sink. Their *mamm* had left the community and gone English after their father's death.

"Rue is an Englisher child," Thomas added. "And our *mamm* is her real Mammi, you know."

"Rue is *your* child," Noah said curtly. "And if you want to raise her right, you'll raise her Amish."

Raising Rue Amish meant keeping her from Englisher influences. Did that include her grandmother?

"Obviously, I'll raise her Amish," Thomas said. "But Mamm also said she wanted to see you—"

"No."

Thomas eyed his brother. This was an old argument. Mamm came back to visit once every so often, and she sent letters, but Noah remained obstinately reserved. And yet, she was their *mamm*. She'd been the one to tuck them in, give them hugs and teach them right from wrong. She was their first love—the beautiful *mamm* who sang the strange Englisher hymns when there was no one else around to hear. When it rained, Thomas could still hear his *mamm*'s soft singing. *Rock of Ages, cleft for me... Let me hide myself in Thee...*

In English.

"She made her choice," Noah said, his voice thick. "She could have stayed for *us!*"

Thomas didn't answer that. He understood his brother's anger, because he felt it, too. When he was fourteen and Noah was fifteen, she'd given them the choice to leave with her, or stay without her. What kind of choice was that? She'd been their *mamm*, and one day she'd told them that that she couldn't continue this way, and their entire world had been thrown upside down. So Thomas could understand the anger in his daughter, because he carried around a fair amount of anger, too. He'd been trying to sort through it during his wild Rumspringa.

There was movement at the top of the stairs, and Mammi and Rue came back down.

Rue was dressed in a nightgown that showed a cartoon princess on the front, and it had little frilly ruffles around the arms. He glanced at his brother—their conversation would have to wait.

"Tell our schoolteacher that she will need a proper nightgown, too," Mammi said.

"Very good," Thomas said, smiling at Rue. "Now, I will sit in the rocking chair, and you will sit on my lap. I will tell you stories, and when your eyes get heavy, you must promise to let them close. Is that a deal?"

"You want to trick me into sleeping," Rue said.

"Yes." He met her young gaze. "That is exactly what I intend to do. With stories."

Rue regarded him for a moment, and she seemed to be deciding what she thought of him. Then she sighed.

"Okay," she whispered. "But I want stories."

Thomas smiled and scooped her up in his arms, then strode into the sitting room. Behind him, he could hear Mammi chiding Noah for having done most of the dishes.

Thomas was a *daet* now. And he had story after story saved up inside him, all meant for his own children one day. These were the stories that formed Amish children—Bible stories, family tales, stories of warning about people they used to know who took a wrong turn and lived to regret it. And tonight, Rue would have her first story.

Thomas settled himself into the rocking chair and Rue curled up her legs and leaned her head against his chest. She smelled of the soap Mammi had used to wash her face and hands, and he gingerly smoothed a hand over her flaxen hair.

"Are we ready, then?" he asked.

Rue nodded mutely.

"Tonight, I will tell you a story about the very first man and woman to live in this world. It was a very, very long time ago, in the days of *In the beginning*. So long ago, that no one remembers just what this first man and woman looked like…"

He would tell her the story of a snake in a garden, and a very tempting piece of fruit that had been forbidden to the inhabitants. That piece of fruit still hung before all the Amish community, just out of reach, just over the fence... And Thomas's own *mamm* had chosen the fruit.

The next morning, Patience dried the last plate from the breakfast dishes and put it into the cupboard. Cheerful sunlight splashed through the kitchen window and over the freshly wiped counters. Outside, she could hear the robins' songs, and she felt a certain excitement inside her that she hadn't experienced in quite some time. It was more than having a job to look forward to, though. And teaching school was definitely something new... But there had been something about Thomas and little Rue that had piqued her interest.

"A child needs a woman's touch," Hannah Kauffman said as she wiped the table. "You're kind to help him."

"The poor thing," Patience said. "This will be a hard adjustment for her."

"Hmm." Hannah straightened. "And for him. Mary and Amos raised him after his *daet* died and his *mamm* left, so I heard all the stories of his struggles as he grew up. I mean, Rachel did come visit, and she sent him letters in between, but it's not the same, is it? No one thought Thomas would come back after he went to live with his *mamm*. And when he did, we all knew there would be baggage. It wasn't just a Rumspringa—it was a boy's chance to spend time with the *mamm* who left him behind. Both of those boys were so heartbroken..."

Patience folded the wet towel and hung it up. "He's been through a lot."

"More than any of us know, I'm sure," Hannah replied, then she batted her hand through the air. "But you go on, now. I can handle the rest. Thomas will be waiting on you."

"Thank you, Hannah," Patience replied. "I'll make it up to you this evening."

It was a cool morning, and as Patience walked down the drive, she could feel fall coming in the air. A couple of leaves had started to turn—only one or two—but it was a hint at things to come.

Trees lined the gravel drive, and their branches stretched overhead, leaves trembling in the morning breeze. Some magpies chattered from the top of one tree, and they were answered by a group of crows—some sort of bird standoff happening above her head. She waved at Samuel Kauffman as she walked past. He was bent over a shovel, harvesting the last of the potatoes from their garden just past the horse stable. There were three draft horses grazing in the pasture beyond, and the animals looked up at her in mild curiosity.

Ruben had owned a property similar to this one, and there had been a time when she'd imagined what it would be like to be his wife, to be mistress of that home, to be the *mamm* calling those *kinner* down to breakfast. She still felt a pang of regret at all she'd given up in a life with Ruben, but she knew it had been the right choice. She wouldn't be able to give him what he truly wanted, and even if he left his offer of marriage on the table after he knew that she couldn't give him babies, she knew he'd be settling. It wasn't the kind of marriage a woman dreamed of, where a man had to lower his hopes in order to be with her.

In some ways, coming to a new community was a fresh start. She didn't know these people, their histories or their families. But the farther one went from home, the more it all looked the same. Amish lives all revolved around the same ideals—marriage, children, farming… A plain life was not an easy life, nor was it excitingly different in another community. Her problems would not change, but at least here in Redemption, she'd have a meaningful job.

When Patience approached the Lapp house, she could hear Rue's crying a good way up the drive. And when she arrived at the door, she knocked twice before it was flung open by a frazzled-looking Thomas. His hair was tousled and from inside she could hear the renewed wails of his young daughter.

"Patience!" he said, stepping back. "You're here."

"I am." She met his gaze questioningly.

"Go!" He gestured inside. "Help me with this!"

Patience swept past him, and she heard the door thunk shut behind her as she headed into the kitchen. The other men seemed to be out doing their chores, because it was only Mammi in the kitchen with Rue, and she was standing at the sink, completely ignoring the meltdown going on in the center of the kitchen floor. She looked up with a mild smile on her face.

"Good morning, Patience," she called, her voice hardly to be heard over the tantrum.

Rue lay there, drumming her heels against the floor, howling her heart out. Patience looked down at her for a moment, then pulled up a chair and sat down on it right next to Rue.

"What happened?" Patience asked.

"We told her that she was getting new clothes," Thomas replied, shrugging helplessly. "And then…this!"

The child continued to wail and pushed herself away from the chair another couple of feet, but when she got no more attention than Patience's watchful eye, her crying lowered in volume until she lay curled up in a ball, sobbing softly. It was then that Patience sat down on the floor next to her and held out her arms.

"Come for a hug, Rue," Patience said softly, and Rue crawled into her lap and leaned her tear-streaked face against Patience's shoulder, then let out a long, shuddering sigh.

"Now," Patience said. "What is the problem, little one?"

"I don't want a new dress," Rue said, her voice trembling. "I don't want it."

"Why not?" she asked.

"I don't want it…"

At this age, Rue wouldn't even know why not, and it likely wouldn't matter. What Rue didn't want was this— a new home, a father she'd never known, a way of life utterly foreign to all the things that used to comfort her.

"We aren't getting a new dress today," Patience said simply.

Rue looked up, startled.

"But Daddy said—"

"We're looking at fabric today. This is fabric—"

She fingered Rue's nightgown between her fingers. "It comes in huge rolls. You'll see them."

"But no dress?" Rue asked.

"No. We're only getting fabric. I have to sew the dress myself. You can watch me. I'll use a needle and thread. Have you ever seen that?"

"No." Rue shook her head.

"It takes some time. But it's fun. And you can see how it works. And you'll be wearing your own clothes while I do it."

"Oh…" Rue wiped her nose across her hand. "I like my clothes."

"They are very nice," Patience said. "Did your *mamm* buy them for you?"

Would mentioning her *mamm* only make this worse?

"Mommy got me this nightgown," Rue said softly, holding it out to look at the picture on the front. "It's a princess nightgown."

"Very pretty…"

"And Mommy got me my unicorn shirt." Rue was looking up earnestly into Patience's face now, and she sensed that Rue desperately wanted someone to understand. "And Mommy got me my pink ruffle socks. And my purple shorts…"

All the clothing that would be taken from her—every item that was most inappropriate for an Amish girl to wear. But it had meaning to Rue because it was connected to the mother she lost, and Patience could suddenly imagine the disapproving looks of every single Amish adult who had looked into her precious suitcase of memories.

"I think I understand," Patience said quietly. "Should I explain it to your *daet*?"

Rue nodded quickly.

"Rue wants to keep her clothes," Patience said, looking up at Thomas.

Thomas stood there for a moment, looming over them, and then he pulled up that kitchen chair next to where Patience sat on the floor with Rue on her lap, and he sat down in it.

"*Yah*, I heard that," he said somberly.

"Her mother bought them, Thomas," Patience said quietly, switching to German. "This is her last connection to the mother she's lost, and I'm sure she knows that we're planning on getting rid of every last stitch of her Englisher clothes."

"*Yah,*" he replied in German. "Of course!"

"It will break her heart," Patience said. "She isn't ready for that."

"No, she's not..." He sighed and rubbed his hands over his face. "I'm so eager to make her Amish that I forget she's not." Thomas looked up, his dark gaze meeting hers. "I will pray on it."

"And in the meantime, can I tell her she keeps the clothes?" Patience asked hopefully.

"In the meantime, yes."

"Your *daet* understands," Patience said, turning to Rue and switching back to English. "And you can keep your clothes. He just wants to give you *more* clothes."

"More?" she asked, and she looked up at her father with such hope in her eyes.

"More," he said solemnly. "Proper Amish dresses for my little Amish girl."

"Am I Amish, Daddy?" she asked.

"Yah," he said. "And I would like it if you called me Daet."

Rue frowned.

"It means *daddy* in German," Patience said.

"I don't like that…" Rue shook her head. "You talk funny."

"Okay," Thomas answered almost too quickly, and Patience had to smother a smile. He was afraid of another meltdown, and right now, she couldn't blame him.

"You're Daddy," Rue said seriously, fixing Thomas with a no-nonsense look of her own. Thomas looked at his daughter for a moment, then sighed.

"For now," he agreed. "I'll be… Daddy."

It was a painful concession, and Patience knew it. Daddies were of the Englisher world, but an Amish father was a *daet.* Tiny children learned to form the word, and it was a tender name, one attached to deep love and emotion. Thomas didn't want to be Daddy, and Patience understood all too well why he wouldn't.

Patience disentangled herself from the girl and boosted her to her feet. "Rue, have you had your breakfast?"

"Yes."

"Have you washed your face and your hands? Did you brush your teeth?"

Mary Lapp dried her hands on a towel at the sink and cast Patience a grateful smile, then held out her hand.

"Come, Rue," Mary said. "Let's get clean so you can see the big rolls of fabric."

It seemed to work, because Rue agreed to trot upstairs with the older woman. Thomas stood up, then held his hand out to Patience to help her to her feet. Patience took his hand, and his grip was warm and solid, calloused from the hard work he did every day. He was strong, and he pulled her easily to her feet.

"You're good with her," Thomas said, releasing her hand.

"I don't know why," Patience said, stepping back. "I don't know anything about Englisher children."

Thomas smiled sadly. "Me neither."

"We'll figure it out," Patience said.

"Gott teaches patience with children. Isn't that what they say?"

"It is." She smiled. "And I'm about to have a whole schoolhouse full of them, so maybe you should feel grateful for just one."

Thomas cracked a smile then, and he laughed softly. "Maybe I should." He jutted his chin toward the door. "I'm going to go hitch up the buggy."

Patience watched as he headed out the side door, and she put a hand over her pattering heart. She wasn't blind to his broad shoulders and warm smile—it would be easier if she were, because it wasn't that she didn't want to marry... She did. But she was going to be a disappointment to whoever tried to court her.

Patience was a teacher and a helpful neighbor. Nothing else. She'd best remember it. Strong hands and broad shoulders didn't change that she wasn't the wife for Thomas.

Chapter Three

The horses trotted along the paved road, the scenery slowly easing past the buggy. Thomas flicked the reins and looked out past the ditch full of weeds and wildflowers, to the fields beyond. Cattle chewed their cud, lying in the long summer grass, and overhead a string of geese beat their wings heading south. These were the last weeks of warmth, and soon there would be frost in the mornings.

"It's a carriage ride!" Rue said, seated between Thomas and Patience on the bench seat.

"A what?" Thomas asked, turning back toward his daughter.

"A princess rides in a carriage!" Rue said. "Like this."

Thomas looked over Rue's head and caught Patience's eye. She shrugged subtly. Rue wasn't raised with dreams of a gleaming kitchen or a neat new dress she'd stitched herself. She'd been raised with grander hopes, it would seem, the kind that elevated one person high above the rest. The Amish saw the danger in that.

Must this child be so foreign from everything he held dear?

Gott, I don't know how to raise her, he prayed in his heart. *She's so...different.*

And she was also his doing. He'd been the one to roam outside the community's boundaries. He'd been the young man who needed to see if his *mamm*'s world might be better, after all. And back then, he'd deeply hoped that it would be, because he missed his *mamm* so much in between her visits, and her letters said very little that meant anything to him. Those who said that a teenager was old enough, that he no longer needed his *mamm*, were dead wrong, because at the age of fourteen, he'd lain in his bed night after night sobbing his heart out, wishing his mother would come back for good.

"Would you like to see our shop, Rue?" he asked.

"What's that?" Rue asked.

"I'm a carpenter. I build things with wood, and I work at Uncle Amos's carpentry shop. We build everything from beds to cabinets to little carved boxes for Englisher women to put their jewelry in."

"A jewel box?" Rue breathed.

"*Yah*, but we Amish don't use them," he said. "We don't have jewelry."

"A princess does," Rue said.

Right. He sighed. This would be a long journey in the making of an Amish girl.

"You could still come see our shop," Thomas said. "Then you'll know where your *daet* works."

Rue looked up at him, silent. It didn't seem to mean much to her.

"Can I hold that?" she asked, pointing to the reins.

Thomas smiled. He couldn't exactly hand the reins over to a four-year-old, but it was a good sign that she wanted to try it herself. This was how children learned—they got curious and wanted to hold the reins.

"Come sit on my knee, and we'll hold the reins together."

The buggy ride into town wasn't a long one. Patience sat quietly the rest of the ride, and he stole a few looks at her over his daughter's head—noticing some details like the faint freckles across her nose and the wisp of golden hair that came loose from under her *kapp*. She was beautiful in that fresh, wholesome way that he'd missed so much when he'd left the community. But he was also feeling attracted to her, and that made him nervous. He needed to focus on his daughter right now, not the new teacher. Besides, Patience was comforting, and that was exactly what drew him to Tina in the city—a search for comfort. His comfort needed to come from his Father in Heaven, not a woman's arms. He'd learned that the hard way.

A couple of farmers, both of whom Thomas knew, looked at him in open curiosity as their buggies passed, going in the opposite direction. Thomas nodded to them, and they nodded back. Word would spread quickly when they started telling their neighbors what they'd seen. Patience could be easily explained, but Rue wearing a striped Englisher sundress would require more. Thomas had a child—a distinctly Englisher child. People would have opinions about that, to be sure.

The town of Redemption was an Amish-friendly town, which meant that the shops all had buggy parking out front, and there were parking lots with hitching posts. Many of the restaurants and stores were Amish owned and operated, including Redemption Carpentry. Englishers traveled from miles around to visit Redemption and buy up the authentic Amish crafts and food. They ordered Amish cabinetry for their homes and stared at the Amish folk with the open curiosity that only Englishers could pull off.

Redemption Carpentry was on Main Street, with a convenient buggy parking area behind the shop. They also had a stable for their horses, and every few days, they'd bring out a new bale of hay and cart out the soiled hay to be used as fertilizer. Even housing horses during business hours took extra work. That was the life of the Amish—putting their backs into the labor and their hearts into Gott.

Next door to their carpentry shop was Quilts and Such, the fabric shop, and after unhitching the horses and settling them with their oats in the stable, Thomas took Rue's hand and they all walked together to the front door. He felt the curious eyes of Amish and English alike sweeping over him. Benjamin Yoder stared in unveiled shock from his seat on his buggy, and his wife, Waneta, leaned forward to get a better look past her husband's chest. *Yah*, he'd have explaining to do.

Thomas pulled open the door to Redemption Carpentry first. He let Patience and Rue go in ahead of him, out of sight from the passersby on the street. He heaved a sigh of relief as the door shut behind him, the soft tinkle of a bell pealing overhead.

"It's you," Amos said, poking his head out of the workshop. They had a small display room for a few finished products, giving customers an idea of the types of furniture they could order. There were some chests of drawers, sections of headboards, wood and stain samples, and a display shelf of ornately carved jewelry boxes.

"Oh..." Rue sighed, immediately drawn to the boxes. "They're so pretty..."

"*Yah*, but why don't you come see where the real work happens?" Thomas said, and he led the way into the back where Noah was working on a bedpost on a gas-powered lathe.

Thomas let them look around. Rue seemed most interested in the curls of wood shavings on the floor, and she collected a few in her hands.

"You have a good business here," Patience said.

"*Yah*. It's doing quite well," Thomas said, and while he wouldn't brag, they were doing more than well. The Englishers loved their work, and with the three of them meeting orders on time every time, they had a reputation for being reliable, as well.

"This is where your *daet* works," Patience said, bending down next to Rue. "He makes all these beautiful things."

"Could I have a jewelry box?" Rue asked, standing up and fixing Thomas with a hopeful look.

"Those are for the Englisher ladies," he said.

"But I'm an Englisher lady!" Rue insisted.

"No, you're an Amish girl," he said. "And I will get you something that you'll love. You'll see."

He glanced at Patience, and she shrugged faintly. There would be plenty of this in the coming weeks and months, he was sure. His daughter wanted an English life—it was what she was born to. He was the one asking her to change everything she'd been raised to be—and for what? For *him*, a father she hardly knew.

Thomas waved to Noah and Amos, then held the door for Patience and Rue to leave the workshop, heading out into the summer warmth once more. As they left the shop, Rue's gaze lingered on their carved boxes. Maybe bringing her here hadn't been the best idea just yet, but he felt like there were pitfalls anywhere they went.

Next door was the fabric shop, and they ducked inside.

"Good morning!"

It was Lovina Glick, the owner of this shop. Thomas often helped her with mucking out the temporary stalls for her draft horses when she was forced to drive her own buggy into town for the day. Normally, her teenaged son drove her and picked her up again in the evening.

Lovina's gaze landed on Rue, and she looked up at Thomas and Patience in surprise.

"Who is this?" she asked in German.

"This is…" Thomas swallowed. "My daughter."

"Your—" Lovina's gaze whipped over to Patience,

and Thomas could see that he'd have to explain right quick.

"My daughter is from my Rumspringa," he said in German, his voice low. "And this here is Patience Flaud—our new schoolteacher. She's completely unrelated."

"Ah…" Lovina came out from behind the counter and nodded slowly. Her gaze flickered up to Thomas's face, and he could see the disappointment there. She'd been a good friend of his *mamm*'s back in the day, and Lovina had stepped up to be a sort of mother figure to them in their own mother's absence. "I don't think I have a right to ask more than that, Thomas. Not now that you're grown." She paused, and again he saw a flood of disappointment in her eyes. "So what do you need, then?"

Her sudden distance stung.

"We need to buy fabric enough to dress her," Thomas said.

"And you'll burn that, I suppose." Lovina's mouth turned down as she gestured to Rue's sundress. "But yes, I understand. She needs to be dressed properly."

Thomas cleared his throat. "We need enough fabric to make—how many dresses?" He turned to Patience.

"Three to start," Patience said. "She'll need more later, of course. But those will need to be warmer for winter."

"Do you want three different colors?" Lovina asked. "Or all the same for now? It might be good for character to keep them the same—take away the temptation to glory in oneself. It's best to quash that early. I've raised four daughters of my own, mind."

That was aimed at Patience.

"All good girls, I'm sure," Patience said with a smile. "I'm glad you can help me to sort this out, then."

Lovina's gaze moved down to Rue once more, and she cocked her head to one side, chewing the side of her cheek. Thomas knew that look from Lovina—that was her look when she was planning on fixing something, and Rue was the problem to be fixed.

Rue squirmed under that penetrating gaze and squeezed Thomas's hand a little bit tighter.

"You'll need a pattern, I take it?" Lovina turned to Patience, Thomas officially out of the conversation as they moved into more technical requirements.

"Yes, a pattern, thread..." Patience moved away with Lovina. "I brought my own needles, and I have some extra hook clasps, but we might need an extra package of those anyway..."

"You're our new teacher, then?" Lovina's voice this time, and Thomas sighed. He was glad Patience was here to take over this womanly task. He wouldn't have known where to start, and Lovina wouldn't have made it easy on him, either. In fact, if they were alone, she might have demanded a few explanations. She'd been more like an aunt in his teens, and she'd take his moral failing personally.

"I like that one..." Rue moved over to a bolt of fabric with a floral pattern, and she smiled up at him shyly.

"No, Rue," Thomas said. "That's fancy."

She didn't know what that meant yet, and he didn't

have the energy to try to explain it to her in a way she'd understand. So he walked with her over to the fabric in solid colors—blue, green, pink, purple. All sober and muted. Rue's gaze kept moving back to the brighter patterns.

"Patience will choose for us," Thomas said.

"Will it be a princess dress?" Rue asked, her eyes brightening.

"No. It is an Amish dress."

"I can be an Amish princess." She beamed up at him, and he simply stared at her, because he had no answers. The Amish didn't have princesses, and he couldn't give her something she'd like better. That was the hard part. He was offering her a life of humble work, of prudence and piety. How could that compare to her fantasies?

The bell tinkled again over the front door, and Thomas looked up to see two more Amish women come inside with two little girls. He knew the women by sight—one was a school friend's older sister. The other was a distant relative of the bishop who had moved to their community when she got married. One of the little girls looked about the same age as Rue, and the girls moved in the direction of the Amish-approved fabrics. The women nodded a friendly hello to him.

The little girls wandered ahead of the women, fingers lingering on the fabrics as they passed them. The smallest girl reached them first, and she startled when she saw Rue, concealed behind some tall bolts of fabric.

"Hi," Rue whispered.

The little girl frowned, and then started to smile when her older sister plucked at her sleeve.

"Stop," her sister remonstrated in German, and tugged her in the other direction. Both girls then turned their backs and headed back toward the women.

"I want to play with her," Rue said, loudly enough to be heard, and it was then that the women took notice. They looked at Rue, up at Thomas, and then steered their girls away from her.

"Englisher child…" he heard one whisper.

"With Thomas Wiebe, though? Who is she?" Their whispers carried, and Thomas felt his stomach clench in anger.

"You know about his mother…" the other woman replied.

And then he couldn't hear anymore, but they cast a couple of sidelong looks in his direction. They wouldn't ask him directly—they didn't know him well enough for that. They'd simply ask anyone else who might know him better if they knew who that Englisher child was.

The Englishers were perfectly acceptable as tourists or as customers, but not as playmates for their children. Thomas knew that full well—part of the reason why Rue desperately needed plain clothing. When he was a boy, he'd learned the same lesson—don't chat with them, don't do anything more than give a quick answer to a question if forced, and never form friendships with other Englisher children. They wouldn't understand the Amish way, and they'd do what Englishers always did—try to find some common ground with which to lure you away from the narrow path.

Englishers were necessary for an income, but dangerous to their way of life. It was a delicate line to walk, and Amish children learned it early.

"Daddy?" Rue asked, her voice carrying. "Daddy?"

Thomas looked down at her, trying not to let his own tension show, but he wasn't sure he managed it. He would not let his daughter think that he was embarrassed of her.

"Yes, Rue?" he murmured.

"I like the one with flowers."

"We don't have dresses with flowers, Rue," he reminded her. "We're Amish."

And when Thomas looked up, he saw the direct stares of both women—aghast and suddenly understanding perfectly. They quietly herded the girls out of the store in front of them, and the bell tinkled as they left.

Judgment felt heaviest when it was deserved.

Thomas came up beside Patience, and she could feel the anger radiating off him. He placed a protective hand on Rue's head, but when she met his gaze, his eyes glittered, and his jaw was clenched. She caught her breath. Had she done something? She'd been focused on choosing cloth—

"It's not you," he murmured, as if reading her mind. "We need to get back. Have you finished choosing things?"

"Yah," she said. "This will do."

She'd chosen a blue color of fabric that would bring out Rue's beautiful eyes, and a soft pink, because she thought that Rue would like it.

"Good." He turned to Lovina and briskly pulled a wallet from his pocket. "How much?"

Patience waited as Thomas paid the bill, pocketed his wallet once more and picked up the bag.

"We'll see you," Lovina said with a smile.

"Yah." Thomas scooped up his daughter's hand. "Let's go now."

"Wait." Lovina picked up a basket of hard candies and lowered it down to Rue's level. "Because you were so good, Rue. You can have two."

Rue's eyes lit up and she took a moment to choose her two candies. Patience looked over at Thomas, searching for a hint of what the trouble was, and the bell over the door tinkled again, another group of Amish shoppers coming inside.

"Thank you, Lovina," Thomas said tightly as Rue picked up her second candy. "Let's go."

Thomas didn't look up as they made their way to the door, but Patience nodded at the women. This would be her community, too, after all, and soon she'd get to know many of these women in kitchens and at hymn sings.

Thomas headed out the door, and Patience had to quicken her pace to catch up. The door swung shut behind them and the warm August air enveloped them once more.

"I was wrong to take Rue to town like this. She looks—" He sighed and changed to German. "She draws attention."

"People will look later, too," Patience pointed out, following his lead in speaking in the language the child wouldn't understand. "They'll get used to seeing her, though."

"It's not just the staring." Thomas led the way around the building toward the buggy parking in the rear. "They pulled their girls away from her."

As they would... But Patience's heart gave a squeeze. Yes, that would sting. Had Rue noticed? She looked down to see Rue watching them in mild confusion. She gave Rue a reassuring smile.

"It was my fault," Thomas said. "I shouldn't have put her in the middle of that kind of scrutiny. We'll go back home and...and..."

"And not be seen," Patience finished for him.

Thomas didn't answer, but he cast her one forlorn look. She'd been right—that was his hope. He just wanted to get her out of the public eye. They approached the buggy, still hitched, and Thomas took the feed bags off the horses.

"For how long?" Patience asked pointedly.

"What?" He ran a hand over the horses' muscular necks, then looked back at her.

"How long will you keep her hidden away at the house with Mary?" Patience asked.

"A woman's place—" he began.

"A girl needs friends," she countered, interrupting. It wasn't right for a woman to cut a man off when he was speaking, but her heart was beating fast. "A girl needs to know people—see people. Yes, her place is in her home, and one day she'll marry and make a home of her own, but if she's treated like a dirty secret—"

"She is *not* a dirty secret!" Thomas snapped back.

"She's a vulnerable little girl and her *daet* has done wrong. I'm trying to protect her."

She knew he was only trying to protect his daughter, and he was right that some proper Amish clothes would make her more presentable…

"Thomas, I'm not saying we shouldn't go home right now. I'm only pointing out that there will be explaining anyway," Patience said. "She will be a surprise, regardless, and as uncomfortable as it is, you will have to tell the story again and again. As soon as she speaks, or can't answer a German question, it'll be clear she's Englisher. There's no hiding that."

"Yah." Thomas sighed. "But once she looks proper with a *kapp* and a dress, will they pull their children away still?"

Patience couldn't answer that. They may very well.

"Daddy?" Rue said, and instead of answering, Thomas picked her up and deposited her on the buggy seat.

"Wait there," he said with a forced smile, and then he turned to Patience again. "I've been the subject of gossip before. My mother left the community when my father died. She couldn't do it alone—walk the narrow path. She said she had friends and family with the Englishers, and she missed them. I had no idea my parents had been converts, but there you have it. She didn't want to marry another Amish widower to provide for us. She said it was…" He swallowed. "She said it was too hard. But she'd raised us Amish, all the same, and she taught us to choose the hard choice, to take the narrow path. She just wasn't willing to do it without Daet."

Patience stared at him, shocked.

"Where did she go?" Patience whispered.

"To a nearby city. My *mamm* had gone to an Englisher college. She has a sister there in the city, and they hadn't seen each other since she and Daet converted—" His voice caught. "My parents had had this whole life we never knew about. I should have guessed with our last name. It's German, but not typically Amish, but I never thought to question it. So my mother went Mennonite on us… Or went back to being Mennonite might be more accurate. Sure she would come visit and she tried to keep up with our lives, but everyone knew she'd left the Amish life. And I had to endure the gossip and the sidelong looks for years afterward. I know what that feels like."

"I'm sorry," she murmured. So he had his own painful history, too…one that linked him to the Englisher world more than she'd ever suspected.

"We need to help Rue fit in as quickly as possible," Thomas said, his voice low. "She needs Amish clothes. She needs to learn a few German words."

"*Yah,*" she agreed. "I'll do my best."

"That's all I can ask."

"Do you see your mother still?" Patience asked.

"Sometimes," Thomas replied. "She still comes to visit from time to time. She's my *mamm*. I suppose I'm still hoping she'll come back for good."

An Englisher mother, and an Englisher child. Thomas was indeed a very dangerous man, and she understood why a community would be cautious. Patience didn't say anything, but she felt the wariness in her own expression.

"I'm Amish!" he said fervently, reading her face. "I was born Amish, I was raised Amish and, given the choice, I was baptized into the church. Rue can be Amish, too. She's young enough to be formed—I was formed into an Amish man, wasn't I? She can learn our ways. We can teach her our language. And given a few years, the community will do for her what they did for me—"

"What's that?" she asked.

"They'll pretend that she's no different." Thomas held out his hand. "We'd best go now."

Patience put her hand in his warm, strong grip and hoisted herself up into the buggy. Rue was staring at her with wide, worried eyes. Understanding the language or not, the child understood the tension. Patience let out a slow breath. She couldn't let Rue shoulder these adult worries.

"Do you like pie?" Patience asked quietly, shooting Rue a conspiratorial smile.

"Yes," Rue said.

Patience settled herself on the opposite side of the girl so that Rue would be in the middle again.

"Good, because I make a wonderful lemon meringue pie. How are you at licking the whisk?"

Rue smiled again, this time more relaxed. Thomas settled himself onto the seat next to his daughter, and he gave Patience a small smile. Their conversation would have to wait…again.

"I'm a good licker!" Rue declared.

"I'm good at licking the whisk, too," he said in mock seriousness. "It might run in the family."

"No, Daddy, it's for me!" Rue complained, and Patience chuckled.

"Your *daet* will be working, Rue. So there isn't much worry that he'll get to the whisk first."

"You never know," Thomas replied with a teasing grin. "I might sneak back, just in time—"

"Daddy, no!" Rue was smiling this time, though.

"A *daet* deserves a treat, too," he joked, and then he flicked the reins and the horses started.

"A *daddy*..." Rue whispered so softly that Patience almost missed it.

This child would wear a plain dress, and she'd eat Amish food, but there was a stubborn spirit in Rue that would not accept an Amish *daet*.

Chapter Four

Patience helped Rue down from the buggy when they got back to the house. She was light—weighing about the same as a large cat. She was thin, and Patience could feel her ribs through that striped sundress. She was a naturally slight child, and Patience felt an urge to feed her—plump her up, if possible.

"Are those more horses?" Rue asked as Patience set her on the ground. Patience looked in the direction Rue was pointing.

"*Yah*, those are more horses," Thomas said, coming around to their side of the buggy. "But that big one—the black stallion, there—he's mean. Real mean. You stay away from the horse corral, okay?"

"Okay…" Rue frowned. "What's a stallion?"

"A boy horse," Patience said.

"How's it a boy?" Rue squinted up at Patience, and Patience chuckled. There were many lessons that a life on a farm gave to children, but this one could wait.

"If that horse were a human, it would wear a straw

hat and suspenders," Patience replied with a smile. "That's how you know."

"Huh." Rue seemed to accept this at face value. "I want suspenders, too."

"Little girls don't wear suspenders," Patience replied. "They wear pretty dresses, and when they get old enough, they get a *kapp*, like mine. You see this *kapp*?"

She tapped the white fabric that covered her bun.

"Can I have one now?" Rue asked. "Instead of suspenders, then?"

Patience looked over at Thomas and found him watching her, instead of Rue. His brows were knit, and when she caught his gaze, he straightened and dropped it.

"You have to get old enough," Thomas said to Rue. "Now, I'm going to unhitch these horses. You go inside with Patience, okay?"

Thomas waited as Patience caught the little girl's hand, then he took the lead horse's bridle and started toward the stable. Rue stared after him.

"You must be very careful around horses, Rue," Patience said, starting toward the house. "*Kinner* have been hurt very badly playing around horses."

There was so much Rue had to learn. She might not be very old yet, but Amish children her age knew all sorts of safety rules. Add to that, Rue would have to catch up on more than their culture, their clothing and their faith. The very foundation of an Amish child's life was obedience. Immediate obedience. From what Patience saw of the Englisher children in town, they weren't raised with the same expectation. Englisher children sassed back, said no when asked to do something, ignored their parents. It was unheard of in Amish communities—*kinner* who behaved like that were very quickly corrected. And they didn't do it again.

As Patience led Rue into the mudroom, she shut the door behind her. The house was silent, and Patience peeked into the kitchen. There were some dishes to be done, and Mary was nowhere to be seen. When Patience glanced into the sitting room, she saw the old woman in a rocking chair, her chin dropped down to her chest and her breath coming slow and deep.

"Mammi is sleeping," Rue said.

"*Yah*, it looks that way," Patience replied. "We have to be quiet to let her rest. In fact, I think it is your naptime, too."

"Naptime?" Rue eyed Patience uncertainly.

"*Yah. Kinner* like you take naps," Patience replied.

"I'm not a *kinner*!" Rue said.

"*Yah*, you are. *Kinner* means children. You're a child."

"Don't call me that," Rue said irritably.

Rue was tired. It had been a long morning, and Patience could only imagine how hard things had been for her recently.

"All right," Patience said softly. "I will call you sugar, then. Is that nicer?"

Rue considered this a moment, and Patience could see the fight seeping out of her.

"I'm not tired," Rue whispered.

"Then you lie on your bed and you think quiet thoughts," Patience replied.

"I don't want to." Rue's lips pressed together, and that

defiant glitter came back to her eye. Patience had a choice
in how she dealt with this, and she debated inwardly for
a moment, then she squatted down to Rue's level.

"What if I lay down next to you?" Patience asked.

Tears welled in Rue's blue eyes and she nodded.
"Okay."

Patience led Rue upstairs, and she found Mary's bedroom with a little cot all arranged next to her bed. Patience doubted that the old woman would mind her bed
being used for a napping little girl, so Patience lifted
Rue up onto the quilted bed top, and then lay down next
to her. Rue let out a shuddering little sigh.

"I'm not tired," Rue repeated.

"I know, sugar," Patience replied, and she took Rue's
hand in hers. "Me, neither. Let's just lie quietly for a
little while. Maybe we'll even shut our eyes a bit."

It didn't take long for Rue to fall asleep, and Patience looked down at the girl with her long, pale lashes
and the pink little lips. That striped sundress looked so
strange against the blue-and-white Amish quilt, and Patience fingered the material. It was soft and stretchy,
unlike the cotton of plain dresses and men's shirts.
Rue needed new clothes—but would she wear them,
or would she fight it? This girl was so small, and sleeping she looked even younger than her four years, but
the spirit in her—she had fight. Downstairs, the side
door banged shut, and Patience eased herself slowly
off the bed. She could hear the steady beat of Thomas's
footsteps on the stairs. She crossed the room on tiptoe,
and when she got to the doorway, Thomas's face appeared around the doorjamb. Her breath caught, and

for a moment they just looked at each other—his dark gaze meeting hers. He was so close that she had to tip her face up, and she could make out the faint stubble on his chin. He was handsome—dare she admit that? And there was something about the way his gaze moved across her face that made her hold her breath. She'd have to get over her way of reacting to him.

Patience put a finger to her lips. Thomas's dark gaze flicked over her shoulder to where Rue lay sleeping.

"Oh…" he breathed, a smile tickling the corners of his lips. "How did you manage that?"

"I'm not sure," she whispered, and they exchanged a smile.

Thomas angled his head toward the stairs and she let out a shaky breath as he turned away.

"Englisher *kinner* aren't raised the same way," Patience said, following him down the stairs.

"Don't I know it," Thomas replied. He headed for a cupboard and pulled down a sealed plastic container, then opened it. "Do you want a muffin?"

"*Yah*. Thanks."

Thomas passed a blueberry muffin to her, then took one for himself. Patience took a bite and swallowed before she continued.

"Englisher *kinner* don't obey like Amish *kinner*. The Englisher parents seem to do more pleading with their *kinner* to make them behave, and quite frankly, it's dangerous on our land."

"You think I'll be pleading?" he asked ruefully.

"I confess, I did a little pleading of my own up there," she replied.

Thomas laughed—a full, open laugh that she didn't expect—and she blinked at him. His dark eyes met hers with a glitter of humor.

"So, I'm not the only one?" Thomas said, shaking his head. "If she were raised plain, she'd already know the rules. It'll take some time."

"And in the meantime, she's not going to know what's dangerous," Patience added. "From fire in the stove to the horses in the corral—this is all completely foreign to an Englisher child. She's an accident waiting to happen."

"That's why you're here, isn't it?" Thomas asked hopefully.

"*Yah,*" she said. "But I don't think either of us knows what she'll get into once she feels more comfortable."

Thomas nodded. "*Yah.* Definitely. Maybe having her play with some *kinner* would help with that. Learning while she plays."

"It's a good idea," Patience agreed. "I don't even remember learning everything I gleaned while playing with my older sisters. Maybe there are some girls who would… I don't know…take her under wing a little."

Thomas looked at her, his expression sobering. "You saw the reaction of the women in the store today."

"*Yah,*" she admitted. "Maybe that was rooted in surprise, though." Eventually, the community would learn who Rue was and why she was here.

"I'll see what I can sort out," he said.

Patience finished the muffin and then wiped the crumbs from her fingers. She went to the sink, put in the plug and looked around for the dish soap.

"Uh… I can do that," Thomas said.

Patience looked up at him, a little embarrassed. "This is women's work."

"I know it's not my place to tell you what needs to be done," Thomas said, his voice low. "But Rue needs dresses, and if you'd be willing to start on that, I can clean up."

"Oh…" She felt the heat hit her cheeks. Had she overstepped somehow?

"We're a houseful of bachelors," Thomas said. "We fend for ourselves a lot. We'll be right proper once we're married, I'm sure, but—" He shrugged.

"*Yah*, well, I can start sewing," Patience said.

As she stepped away from the sink, Thomas pulled a bottle of dish soap from the cabinet and squirted it into the running water. He rolled his sleeves up past his elbows and looked around himself for a moment, then started gathering the dirty dishes. He looked…practiced. He'd spent time with the Englishers… Was this his time away shining through?

For the next few minutes, Patience cut out the paper pattern for a little dress, then laid out the cloth and began pinning the pattern in place. Mammi's sewing basket was in the corner, so Patience made use of it. Girls' dresses were simple enough to sew, and they left lots of room for a child to grow, too. She'd helped her sisters make all sorts of clothes for her nieces and nephews over the years, so her hands knew the work.

But as she worked, she caught herself looking up at the quiet man who continued to wash, dry and put away the stack of morning dishes.

"I know that you spent time with the Englishers," she said after some silence. "I shouldn't be trying to inform you of how they raise their *kinner*."

"*Yah*. I went there to live with my *mamm* for my Rumspringa and stayed for three years. I'm twenty-four now, so I've been home for a while," he replied. "But they're different, the Englishers. They keep to themselves. You don't see as much as you think you will about how their families work. The young people spend time together, and the older people have their friends... The different generations don't come together very often."

That seemed sad—and lonely. All the same, a woman like her who wouldn't be raising children of her own might fit into an Englisher system a little easier than she would here with her own people. She wouldn't ask about that, though. It wouldn't be right to show curiosity about the Englishers. Still... He'd loved an Englisher girl, hadn't he? Obviously they weren't so strange and different to *him*.

Thomas seemed to feel her eyes on him, and he turned. She felt the heat hit her face and she dropped her attention to the pattern on the fabric. Was that jealousy she'd just felt?

"I had a choice," he said quietly. "I could stay with my *mamm* and live an Englisher life, or I could come back. It wasn't easy. Your home, your life... Your mother is supposed to be a part of that, isn't she?" He waited, as if he expected her to answer, and when she didn't, he went on, "But I'm Amish. And I came back. I'll be Amish until I die."

"I wasn't questioning your dedication," she said.

"I thought it should be said," he replied.

"Do you miss your *mamm*?" she asked quietly.

Thomas pressed his lips together, then nodded. "*Yah*. Of course."

But he was living away from her. An Amish family got together with all the grandparents, aunts and uncles and cousins regularly. Even coming out here to teach school, Patience knew she'd go back to visit her family at Christmas, and to help her *mamm* with all the Christmas baking. Would Thomas have his *mamm*'s cooking to look forward to come Christmas?

Thomas let the water out of the sink and wrung out the cloth. He hung it over the tap neatly.

"I'd best get some work done here at home," he said. "I'll be going back to the shop tomorrow, so…"

"*Yah*, of course," she replied.

Thomas nodded, then headed past the table, his fingers skimming over the tabletop next to the spread-out fabric as he passed her. She watched him disappear into the mudroom, and a moment later the door shut behind him.

There was a rustle at the doorway to the sitting room and Patience looked up to see Mary standing there. Her eyes looked bleary from sleep, and she patted at her hair, checking for any loose strands.

"I must have dozed off," Mary said. "I'd better get to the dishes."

"Thomas did them," Patience replied.

"Did he?" Mary's face pinked. "That boy… They're

treating me like I'm old, you know. What is that you're doing, dear?"

"I'm starting on a dress for Rue," Patience replied.

"Well, let me help, then," Mary said. "I can cut out the cloth still. I'm not as good with the stitching anymore, but—"

"That would be wonderful, Mary," Patience replied with a smile. "Before the day is out, I want her to have at least one proper dress."

Mary came to the table, and pulled out a chair. She reached for the shears, and Patience passed them over.

"She wasn't a bad woman," Mary said, setting to work. "Thomas's *mamm*, I mean. She wasn't a bad woman, just a sad one. She knew how to be Amish with her husband, but she hadn't been raised in our ways, and she didn't know how to do it without him. She couldn't change who she was."

Patience met the old woman's gaze. Did Mary guess at how much Patience was judging the woman who'd left her sons behind? She didn't answer, and Mary didn't say anything further.

There was a dress to be made—an Englisher child to be made over into a plain one. Like her grandmother, Rue had started out an Englisher. Was there any real hope that that this child would stay Amish in the long run?

Two hours later, Thomas came out of the stable with a wheelbarrow full of soiled hay. Sweat beaded on his forehead, and he paused to pull out a handkerchief and wipe his face. The sun shone warm on his shoulders and he pushed his hat up on his forehead as he looked toward the house. It was a bit of a relief to have a young woman around for Rue's sake, but also a little unnerving. They were used to their ways in this house—bachelor men living with one old woman whom they all secretly went out of their way to take care of.

If only this schoolteacher were a little less attractive. He wouldn't be the only one to notice how beautiful she was. His older brother, Noah, certainly would, and Uncle Amos wasn't exactly dead yet, either. Except Amos was legally married still, so his days of courting were past.

And yet, it was silly to be feeling competitive over a woman who was clearly uncomfortable with all the untraditional parts to Thomas's heritage. Englisher convert parents, a *mamm* who didn't stay, an Englisher daughter of his own… Thomas wasn't going to have an easy time of finding a woman—some might see him as a threat to the very fiber of their community.

He dumped the load of soiled hay on the manure pile, and put the wheelbarrow back under the buggy cover where they kept it. The side door opened and Rue appeared on the porch. She stared at him somberly.

Amish *kinner* helped the adults and learned through chores. Work was how a family bonded, and while looking at her in those Englisher clothes was slightly jarring still, she could help with some little jobs.

"You're awake now, are you?" Thomas called.

"Patience tricked me into sleeping," Rue said, leaning against the rails.

"How did she do it?" he asked. Because he might need to use the same "trick" later.

"I don't remember, but it was a trick," Rue replied.

Thomas chuckled. "Well, if you're up now, you could help me with the chickens."

"I can help?" She perked up at that.

"*Yah.* Come on, then. We'll get the eggs. Go ask Mammi for the bucket and bring it out."

Rue disappeared back into the house and Thomas pulled off his work gloves, slapped them against his leg and tucked them into his back pocket. The screen door opened again, and Rue came out, dragging a blue plastic bucket half as big as she was. Patience held the door for her, letting her do the lugging on her own. He couldn't help but let his gaze linger on Patience as she smiled down at his daughter.

"Carry it on down to your *daet*," Patience said cheerily. "And when you're done with the chickens, your dress will be finished."

He dragged his gaze away from her—staring wasn't appropriate behavior.

"Patience is making a dress, Daddy!" Rue hollered as she thumped the bucket down the stairs. "And it's pink!"

By the time she got to him, she was breathing hard, and he bent down and picked up the bucket by the handle.

"Pink, you say...?" he said, and he started toward the chicken coop, Rue trotting along next to him.

"I don't want it," Rue said.

"I know," he replied. "But it's just an extra dress."

"I don't need more," she countered.

The chicken coop was quite large, since Amos wanted his chickens to have space to move about. There was an outside space where they could run and scratch that was portioned off with chicken wire, and then the whitewashed coop where the nesting boxes were.

"Now, you've got to watch for the rooster," Thomas said. "You just stick close to me, and I'll deal with him."

"Why?" Rue asked.

"He's protecting his hens. So he tries to show you that he's boss. You can't let him be boss."

Rue looked up at him, wide-eyed. "Is he naughty?"

"Yah," he replied. "He's very naughty."

"Do you punish him?" Rue asked.

Thomas laughed. "You can't punish a chicken, Rue. They aren't very smart. One of these days, we'll eat him, and then I'll get a new rooster."

"You can't just eat someone for being naughty!" Rue retorted.

"He's not a someone. He's a chicken!" Thomas said, stopping short and looking down at her. "That's where your chicken comes from on your plate, you know."

"What's his name?" Rue asked plaintively.

"He doesn't have a name. He's a chicken." Thomas shook his head. Not only was she an Englisher child, but she was an Englisher child raised in the city. "Rue, don't worry. I won't let him peck you. He'll be fine."

Thomas started toward the coop again, Rue in tow.

"He won't be fine if you eat him!" she said, tramping along behind him. "I'm going to name him Toby."

"You can't name him Toby," Thomas said, opening the coop door.

"Why not?"

"It's not an Amish name," Thomas said. "Besides, we don't name chickens. It's very awkward to eat a chicken you named."

"Daddy, you can't eat Toby."

She hadn't even met the silly bird yet, and she'd grown attached. This was not an argument he'd win, he could tell. "Come on inside, Rue."

The door shut behind them, and Rue wrinkled her nose at the smell.

"*Yah*, chickens smell, too," Thomas said with a low laugh. "Now come on, we're going to get the eggs and put them in the bucket—but very carefully. We don't want to break them, okay?"

"Okay…"

For the next few minutes, Thomas took her around to the nests, pushing his hand under the ruffled hens to retrieve eggs. He handed an egg to Rue, and she cautiously put it in the bucket.

"The eggs are warm," Rue said.

"*Yah*, they start out that way," he agreed.

The rooster eyed them with beady, mistrusting eyes. But he knew Thomas well enough that if he came at him with his spurs and beak, he'd get a boot. Later this evening, Thomas would come back and clean out all the wood shavings and put in some fresh ones to make the coop smell clean again, but it was always a challenge because Thomas couldn't turn his back on that bird. The rooster lowered his head and fluffed up his neck, and his wings came out.

"No, you don't," Thomas said, and he picked up a

wooden switch and flicked it at the bird. The rooster backed off for the moment.

"Why is he mad?" Rue asked, accepting another egg to put in the bucket.

"Because he's a rooster," Thomas said. "And he wants to keep the hens to himself. He's a jealous, feathery little fiend."

"He needs a hug, maybe," Rue said.

Thomas looked down at her, bewildered. "Rue, never hug a chicken, okay? That rooster will hurt you. He doesn't want a hug."

Rue didn't look convinced of that, and he sighed. When they gathered the last of the eggs, including three that had been laid on the top of a beam, Thomas nodded toward the door.

"All right, let's go out now," Thomas said.

"Goodbye, Toby…" Rue said softly, and Thomas pulled the door tight shut behind them. The bright sunlight shone off Rue's blond head and she hopped along next to him as he carried the bucket of eggs back toward the house.

When they got inside, Thomas lifted Rue up so that she could reach the sink, and with one hand he helped her soap up her hands, while he held her under his other arm, like a calf. When she was clean, he washed his own hands, then they dried them and headed into the kitchen.

Patience sat at the table, a mound of fabric in her lap that she was clipping some stray threads from. She lifted it and shook it out, and he saw a small pink cape dress. His heart gave a grateful squeeze.

"I see you brought us eggs," Mammi said with a smile.

"It's a lot of eggs," Rue said.

"We have a lot of baking to do," Mammi replied. "Cakes, and buns and bread and pies..."

"Can we share some with Toby?" Rue asked.

Mary and Patience both looked toward Thomas questioningly.

"She named the rooster," he said helplessly.

"That ratty, ugly, nasty rooster?" Mary asked with a shake of her head.

"His name is Toby, and I love him," Rue declared. "Don't call him those things! Call him pretty and sweet... Call him Toby!"

"Come with me into the other room, Rue," Patience said. "I'm going to get you into your new dress and you can show your *daet*."

Patience took Rue's hand and they headed down the hallway together.

"I think Toby needs to be hugged..." Rue's little voice was saying as they disappeared into the laundry room.

Thomas rubbed his hands over his face, then shook his head. "She's so—"

"English?" Mary asked, but her tone was full of humor.

"Yah," he said. "She's English. To the bone, it would seem."

"I thought we were going to eat that rooster," Mary said.

"I'm not sure we can now," Thomas replied. "She decided she loved it sight unseen. I have no idea why."

Mary chuckled. "Welcome to being a *daet*, Thomas. Your whole world goes upside down. And *kinner* seldom make perfect sense. They are confusing little bundles of personality and willfulness. Gott grows us more through parenting than He does through anything else."

"Yah…" Thomas had heard the same thing repeated over and over again, but he was getting a firsthand view of exactly how true it was.

From the other room, he could hear Patience's soft tones… It was different having her here—but it was different having Rue here, too. Suddenly this house full of bachelors had more female presence to even them out. But he found himself straining to hear one particular voice—the soft, reassuring tones of their schoolteacher.

Rue emerged into the kitchen again first, clad in that small pink dress that fit her perfectly. Her feet were bare, and her hair was tangled, and she looked up at Thomas irritably.

"Very nice," Thomas said with a smile. "You look like an Amish girl now."

"I'm not an Amish girl," Rue replied.

Patience came up behind her, holding Rue's folded sundress. Patience looked as cool and neat as a spring morning, except for one tendril of honey-blond hair that had come loose from her *kapp* and fell down the side of her face. There was something soothing about their new schoolteacher. She calmed him, at least.

"Will it do?" Patience asked.

"It'll more than do," Thomas said. "It's perfect."

Patience smiled at that, her own blue gaze meeting his for just a moment, before she seemed to feel the hair against her face and she tucked it back up under her *kapp*. Then she turned toward the table with the scraps of cloth, bits of thread and the open sewing box and started to clean up. Thomas's gaze moved back to his little girl.

"Thank you for this, Patience," he said quietly.

"*Yah.* You're welcome. It's no trouble," she replied. "I'll make another one tomorrow."

But it wasn't about the trouble, it was about the transformation. If this little wildcat could be made to look Amish, then it was a step in the right direction. Because while he couldn't help the start she'd had in life, he could try to make up for it now.

Could he raise his daughter to become like this—an Amish woman who loved this life? Could he give his daughter a community, a place to belong and work that made her happy?

Maybe... But when he looked over at his daughter, she was looking down at her dress balefully.

"She looks very proper," Thomas said. Not happy, but at least she looked Amish.

"I think she looks like you, Thomas," Patience said, and then she moved past him toward the cloth scrap bag.

Hopefully that wasn't a comment on his expression, because Rue looked about as sweet as that rooster outside right now. Rue needed more than genetics to help her settle in. She needed a new mother, and some brothers and sisters to nail her down. Because her link to her *daet*, as well-intentioned as he was, wouldn't be nearly enough.

Chapter Five

The next day, Patience worked on a second dress for Rue with Mary's help in some of the hemming and the cutting. Between the two of them, the work went smoothly, and Rue played outside in the garden, picking the tender, tiny pea pods and crunching on them whole. She looked toward the chicken coop, standing, staring thoughtfully, and then gathered a few more pea pods and headed over there.

Patience watched her through the kitchen window.

"What's she up to?" Mary asked.

"Feeding peas to the chickens," Patience replied.

"Ah." Mammi smiled at that. "At heart, *kinner* are all the same. They like to eat and feed things."

Patience chuckled at that. She'd find out a lot more about *kinner* when she had a classroom filled with them from the first grade through to the eighth. She was used to caring for her nieces and nephews, and most young Amish women had plenty of practice in taking care of little ones. But this would be a whole new challenge.

Last night, sleeping in the upstairs bedroom of the Kauffman house, Patience had lain awake wondering about the strange story surrounding Thomas. If she hadn't been told what had happened, he would seem like a regular Amish man to her. He loved his work, he seemed dedicated to the Amish way of life and there was nothing about him that stood out as different. And yet, everything about him was different.

But he wasn't the only one with a peculiar story, it would seem. These men were bachelors living together, or so she'd been told. And most had been married before.

Patience reached for an iron staying hot on the stove and smoothed it over a finished seam on the cape of the dress. The kitchen was overly warm because of the stove, and they had all the windows propped open, and the side door, too, trying to get some cooler air moving through.

Mary was making sure the stove did double duty, and she had some meat pies baking in the oven alongside some potatoes and some flatbread cooking on the stove top—all to feed the hungry men who'd be home soon for their dinner.

"What happened to Amos?" Patience asked. "He has a beard. Did his wife die?"

Mary looked up from her work, using her bare fingers to pluck up some flatbread and flip it on the pan.

"That's a sad story," Mary replied. "She didn't die. Her name is Miriam, and she left Amos after their first year of marriage. She went back home to her family in another community."

"Why?" Patience asked.

"They weren't happy," Mammi replied. "They were both stubborn, and we all told him when he set his sights on her that it wouldn't end well. She was too well off, and Amos barely had two nickels to rub together." Mammi paused, thoughtful. "We aren't supposed to focus on money, but it does make a difference. He could afford a little cottage on the corner of someone else's land. And her *daet* owned two farms free and clear. They butted heads a lot, and Amos was more fiery-tempered back then."

"Oh…" Patience sighed. "That's sad."

"*Yah*, it is," Mammi replied. "And she broke his heart when she left him. But now they're both living their own separate lives, and… It is what it is."

"Isn't it worth patching it up?" Patience asked.

"He tried once. He went out to see her *daet*, but her *daet*'s a proud man, and he told Amos that if he wanted his support in bringing Miriam back home, then he'd better prove himself a better provider. That insulted him deeply, and he just couldn't forgive it."

"And she'd rather live without a husband?" Patience asked.

"Well… The way I heard it, she'd rather live without the fighting," Mary replied. "A marriage takes two, dear, and she wasn't used to Amos's ways any more than he was accustomed to hers. There is always another side to the story."

Patience brought the dress back to the table where she had better light and sat down to begin hemming the sleeves.

"Noah and Thomas came to stay with us because we had the room," Mary went on. "Besides, the boys were both working with Amos in the carpentry shop, so they all knew each other well. When their *mamm* jumped the fence, they had the choice to go with her, or to stay with us. They both chose to stay."

"Is he like a *daet* to them, then?" Patience asked.

"More like an older brother," Mammi replied. "He's protective. He gives advice. They're as close to *kinner* as he'll ever get, I suppose."

How many women had just walked away from the men in his household? Amos's wife abandoned him, and Noah and Thomas's mother did the same. From what she could see of these men, they were kind and decent—and lonesome. Men needed some nurturing as much as anyone—maybe even more so when they seemed the strongest.

Mary rapped on the kitchen window. "Rue, stay away from there!"

"What's she up to?" Patience went to the door and saw Rue stop short at Mary's call. Rue had been headed toward the horse corral. She looked just like any other Amish girl now in her little pink cape dress, except her hair was shorter, with bangs in the front, and she still wore her flip-flops.

"Come back inside, Rue!" Patience called.

Rue turned and came back toward the house, dragging her feet and glancing over her shoulder a couple of times.

"I wanted to see the horses," Rue said as she came up the steps.

"The horses aren't for playing," Patience replied. "They could squish you."

Rue sighed and came indoors, her little flip-flops making a slapping sound against the bottoms of her feet.

"You can take those off," Mary said. "Go barefoot."

Rue stepped out of the sandals and walked away from them.

"Put them in the mudroom, dear," Mary said. "We all have to pick up after ourselves, or else we'll have nothing but mess and confusion."

Rue looked up at Mary mutely, her eyes suddenly misting.

"It's okay," Patience said, and she scooped up the sandals herself, depositing them in the mudroom next to the men's big boots. "Are you hungry, sugar?"

Rue smiled faintly at the endearment. "Yeah…"

"Come have a taste of some flatbread," Mary said. "Come on, it's okay. Come try it. Supper is ready soon. We're just waiting on the men."

Outside, she heard the sound of a buggy's wheels crunching over gravel and the cheerful rumble of deep voices. The men were home. Rue came dancing across the room, a piece of flatbread in one hand, and she stood in front of the closed screen door, waiting.

Patience gathered up her work and put it into a sewing basket. The dress was nearly finished—two more hems and it was ready to be worn. When she'd cleared her work off the table, the door opened and Amos came inside.

"Something smells wonderful, Mammi," Amos

boomed out, and then he looked down at Rue. "Hello, Rue."

Rue stared at him in wide-eyed silence.

"You can't be so noisy with little girls," Mary said, shaking her head. "Now, you wash up and sit down, Amos."

Amos cast Patience a rueful look, but did as Mary asked of him. Noah was next to come inside, and he squatted down to say hello to Rue.

"I like that dress," Noah said with a smile.

"It's okay," Rue said. "I can run in it."

"Well, I like it," Noah replied. "Did you know that I'm your uncle?"

Rue shook her head.

"Well, I am. I'm Uncle Noah. And when Uncle Amos gets too noisy, you just tell me, okay?"

Rue shot a look toward Mary, and Patience chuckled.

"Mammi can take care of that, too, I'm sure."

Noah grinned in Patience's direction and stood up to go wash his hands when Thomas came inside. His gaze moved over the kitchen, stopping at Patience for a moment, and he gave her a small smile. He had already washed, and he had a package in his hand—a white plastic bag.

"I brought something," Thomas said, turning to Rue.

"For me?" Rue whispered.

"*Yah*, for my little girl," Thomas said, and handed her the bag.

Rue opened it and pulled out a cloth doll wearing a purple Amish dress and a bonnet. She looked at it for a moment, then tears welled in her eyes.

"No," she whispered.

"What's wrong, Rue?" Patience asked, bending down next to her.

"No!" Rue said. "I don't like it! I don't want it!"

"It's a beautiful doll, sugar," Patience said. "I think it's lovely."

"I don't!" Rue shook her head. "I want a Barbie. I want a Barbie with long hair and pretty dresses."

A Barbie… Patience didn't even know what that was. When she looked up, she saw Thomas standing there awkwardly, his gift rejected. He took off his hat and ran a hand through his hair.

"What's a Barbie?" Patience asked.

"An Englisher toy. The *kinner* love them…" Thomas put his hat on a hook and heaved a sigh. "I'm sorry, Rue. We don't play with Barbies here."

Tears spilled down Rue's cheeks, her lower lip trembling, and Patience scooped her up in her arms, cuddling her close. Rue pushed her wet face into Patience's neck and let out a trembling sigh. The discarded doll lay on the floor next to the crumpled plastic bag.

Thomas looked at her with a helpless expression on his face. He bent down and picked up the doll and bag. He wadded the bag up in one hand, and placed the doll on the corner of the table.

"I thought I'd try," he said, his voice low.

"Give it time," Patience said. "She'll play with it eventually."

Maybe. Unless she decided to blame all things Amish for the depth of her loss.

"Yah." Thomas lifted his hand as if he wanted to pat

his daughter's back, and then he let it drop. "Would you stay for dinner, Patience?"

"I don't mean to intrude on your family time," Patience said.

"No, it would be…helpful," Thomas replied. "If you wanted to, at least."

"Sure," she replied. "If it would help."

Thomas picked up the doll and carried it into the other room. He looked down at the fabric body, with the little purple cape dress that was a perfect imitation of the dresses worn by the women in their community. The doll had brown hair made of string that disappeared behind a crisp white *kapp*. Lovina Glick had sold it to him—one of several she had for sale. There had been one doll with blond hair like Rue's, but she'd been wearing a black dress, and Thomas thought she'd like a purple dress better.

He'd shown the doll to Noah and Amos, and they'd thought it was a great idea, too. He'd wanted to make his daughter happy, and her reaction cut him more deeply than he wanted the others to know.

When he came back into the kitchen, Rue was sitting next to Noah at the table, and Patience was in the kitchen with Mammi.

Noah gave Thomas a sympathetic shrug, silently offering some emotional support.

"Rue, why don't you come help me?" Mammi called. "We need someone to wash carrots. Do you think you could do that?"

Rue looked over hesitantly.

"The water is nice and cold," Patience added. "It would feel so nice on your hands."

Rue climbed down from her chair and headed over to where the women were working, and Thomas met his brother's gaze.

"I asked her about the doll," Noah said. "She says she likes the rooster better."

Thomas smiled at that and shook his head. "She's a stubborn one."

"A lot like her *daet*, might I add," Amos said, coming to the table with a stack of plates. "You were never one to settle into anything without a struggle. Look at what it took to get you home and Amish again."

Thomas had to admit that was true. He'd had to go out there and make his own mess of mistakes before he could see that the Amish life was the one for him. So maybe expecting a more submissive personality from his own daughter wasn't realistic. That possibility was also daunting. It was one thing for a man to accept his own mistakes in his journey home, but quite another to face the likelihood of his daughter doing the same.

"I'm going to pick three more carrots!" Rue said, running for the door. Thomas watched her slam outside, then looked over at Mary and Patience.

"Oh, she's fine," Mary said. "It's good to have young ones help. Besides, they have more energy."

Mary looked out the window, then rapped on the glass.

"No, Rue! Not those! Those are cucumbers!" Mammi called. "Over more…more…by the tree, Rue! Yes!"

Patience stood at the counter mashing potatoes, and

he saw the smile tickle her lips. She glanced up and met his gaze, her eyes glittering with humor.

"She's gone to see the chickens…" Mary sighed, turning back to the stove. "The Englishers really don't teach their *kinner* how to fetch things, do they?"

Patience laughed. "She's new at this."

Mary muttered something Thomas couldn't make out, and he chuckled. "She'll come back with carrot tops, you know."

Four-year-old Englishers didn't know how to pull carrots, and he got up from his seat and headed to the side door to see how she was doing. But when he got there, all he could see was a single, dirt-covered carrot, several more carrot tops, as he'd predicted, but no Rue. She wasn't in the garden or at the chicken coop, either. His heart sped up, and as he scanned the property, he spotted her over by the corral.

"Rue!" he called.

Rue looked over her shoulder, but didn't stop moving closer to the horses. The unbroken stallion was closest to the fence, and Thomas's heart stuttered to a stop.

"Rue!" he barked, sounding a whole lot gruffer than he even intended. The girl stopped. She didn't turn, though, and she seemed undecided about what she was going to do. He didn't have time to find out.

Thomas headed out of the house and then strode across the yard in Rue's direction. She saw him coming, and instead of turning back, she climbed up on the fence and thrust her hand out toward the stallion.

The horse, whether in response to the unexpected hand, or to Thomas's thundercloud of a face, shied back just as Thomas arrived and slipped an arm around Rue's waist, plucking her neatly off the fence.

Rue set up a howl, and he stalked back toward the house, his daughter under his arm. His heart was hammering hard in his chest, and when he got to the side door, he was met with four mildly surprised adults staring at him.

"She went for the horses," he said, putting Rue down. She immediately collapsed into a pile, wailing her heart out.

"That's very dangerous," Amos said. "And she didn't listen."

"I'm telling you," Mary said, fire in her eyes. "It's those Englishers and their lazy way of bringing up their *kinner*. No discipline!"

But Thomas wasn't actually convinced of that. Rue couldn't be blamed for not knowing the dangers around her. She hadn't been raised with horses and chickens and carrots that came from the ground. She knew about cars, crosswalks and not to talk to strangers. Not much of that applied here—not on a daily basis, at least.

And yet, he was the *daet* here, and everyone was looking to him to decide on what should be done. It wasn't just a misunderstanding—she'd willfully disobeyed. She had to be disciplined, but the prospect of doing so clamped a vise around his chest.

"Come, Rue," he said firmly, picking her up and setting her on her feet. Then he led her out of the kitchen and up the stairs.

Rue continued to cry, but he could tell at this point that her crying was mostly put on for effect, and she watched him with teary curiosity as he led her up to the bedroom she shared with Mary.

He set her on the side of Mary's bed, and she sniffled and wiped her eyes.

"Why didn't you obey?" he asked, sitting down on the edge of the bed next to her.

Rue didn't answer.

"There are rules in this home, Rue," Thomas said slowly. "And they are going to be different rules than what you had with your *mamm*. You won't have to worry about the same things. There will be no day care, or holding a rope, or electrical sockets. But there are dangers here, too. And those horses are dangerous. They could crush you."

"I wanted to hug him," Rue said.

Thomas felt that rise of frustration. Why did she have to be so different? Why couldn't she see reason? Obviously, small *kinner* weren't going to be as rational as when they got older, but even the little Amish *kinner* knew better than to try to hug horses in a corral. They learned quickly from the adults around them.

"He could have bitten you," Thomas added. "That horse has very big teeth."

Rue pulled her fingers back into a small fist and licked her lips.

"You must never disobey like that again," Thomas said firmly. "What did your *mamm* do when you got in trouble at home?"

Rue blinked up at him.

"Did you get sent to your room? Did you get put in a corner?"

Rue didn't answer. Had she been corrected at all?

He looked around the room. He had to make a point, or else she might get herself badly injured next, all because of uncurbed defiance.

His gaze landed on her suitcase, and he rose to his feet and went over to it. Rue's gaze followed him, and as he opened the case, her entire body lurched forward.

"No!" Rue shouted.

Thomas pulled her pajamas out of the case and laid them on the edge of the bed.

"I am going to leave you your pajamas, but I am taking the rest of your old clothes until you can listen better. When you are able to do as you're told and obey the first time, you can have your suitcase back."

Rue's eyes stayed fixed on the case, filling with tears. The color had gone out of her cheeks and her hands trembled. "No…"

He could already feel how deeply this was cutting the girl, but he'd made a decision and he had to stand by it. *Kinner* didn't benefit from parents who swayed with the wind, and she had to learn to listen, if only for her own safety.

"*Yah*, Rue," he said firmly, picking up the case. "Now, you will come downstairs for your dinner."

Rue turned her back on him and laid her head down on Mary's pillow with a shuddering sigh. She didn't cry again, but she didn't turn to look at him, either, and he stared at that tiny form, filled with his own misgiving. Was this going too far?

But he'd made his decision, and he couldn't go back on it now, so taking the suitcase with him, he left the room and deposited it inside his closet. When he came back down the hall, he looked in Mary's room again and Rue hadn't changed her position. She lay on the bed, so small that she barely took up a corner, her entire body curved around her knees, and her tangled blond hair spread across the white cotton of Mary's pillow.

"You can come down for dinner, Rue," he repeated.

"No," Rue said.

So he carried on down the stairs. The meal was on the table, and Amos and Noah were both seated already. Patience was just putting a bowl of gravy on the table when she spotted him.

"Is she coming to eat?" Mary asked.

"No, she doesn't want to," Thomas replied.

"What did you do?" Noah asked. "A lecture?"

"A lecture, and—" He swallowed. "I took her suit-case."

"Just as well," Mary said, coming to the table. "Those clothes are inappropriate for our girls anyway. If she's going to be one of us, those clothes had to go. The sooner the better."

Patience didn't speak, but there was a tightness around her mouth that betrayed an opinion, and she dropped her gaze.

"Let's pray," Amos said, bowing his head. "For this food we are about to eat, make us truly grateful. Amen."

"Amen," the rest of them murmured, and there was the rustle of food being passed and the clink of dishing up.

"Was I wrong?" Thomas asked, turning toward Patience.

"You're her *daet*," she said simply.

"But was I wrong?" he pressed. "I know what Mammi thinks. I want to know what you think."

Patience accepted the bowl of mashed potatoes from Noah and handed them to Thomas.

"Those clothes are more than something she likes," Patience said, her voice low so that only he could hear her. "They are her last link to her dead *mamm*."

He knew that, and he hated the way she'd caved in like that when he took them. He wasn't going to burn them—and he knew plenty of men who might in the same situation.

"If she'd liked the doll, I might have taken that away. But something had to be done."

"I agree…"

"Any ideas?" he asked.

Patience shrugged weakly. "She's lost too much. I don't know. Maybe other *kinner* to play with—to see how they're expected to behave—might help."

And that seemed to be the only answer that kept coming back—she needed other *kinner* in her life, and the sooner the better. If he was already married, there would be siblings, but as it was, he'd have to find her some playmates one way or another.

Thomas accepted a plate of chicken from Mary and took a leg, then passed it to Patience. She took some white meat and passed it along.

"Ben Smoker asked if one of us would help him with a broken gate tomorrow," Amos said.

"I could do it," Noah said. "When does he want us to come?"

"In the morning," Amos replied.

But the timing was just too perfect. Thomas needed to show Rue other *kinner* so that she could see that their way wasn't some random, cruel list of rules to follow. She had to see that others were like them, too. And the Smokers had five girls, twelve and under.

"What if I went?" Thomas said. "I could bring Patience and Rue with me, and Rue could play with some *kinner*. It would be good for her. She might see how another family runs."

Amos shrugged, and looked over at Noah.

"*Yah*, I don't mind that," Noah replied. "I didn't want to get behind on that bedroom set that's due to be finished next week, anyway."

"Would you be willing to come along?" Thomas asked Patience.

Patience nodded, and from the stairs, there was a small, shaky voice. "I'm hungry."

They'd all been speaking German up until now, and Thomas looked up to see Rue standing there, her eyes red from tears, and looking so small that his heart nearly broke.

"Come have your dinner, then," Thomas said, patting the stool next to him. "It's chicken."

Rue froze, and he could almost see the cruel possibilities running through her little, tousled head.

"It's not Toby," he clarified.

"Oh, good…" Rue sighed, and she came up to the stool and stared at it.

"Here—" Thomas lifted her onto her seat. When

she was settled, Thomas and Patience both set to filling her plate.

"Now, eat up," Thomas said.

And in those words, he meant so much more—he wanted to say that he loved her already, and that he wanted to keep her safe. He wanted to say that he was sorry that he had to punish her, and that he was only trying to teach her the right way.

But he couldn't say all that, so instead, he gave her a little extra gravy.

Chapter Six

The next morning, Thomas flicked the reins as the horses got into their pace, trotting down the paved road, their hooves clopping cheerfully. Patience sat across from him, with Rue between them, scooted forward so her legs could hang normally. This would help—he was sure of it.

He'd been praying last night about his predicament, and community was the answer to all of an Amish man's troubles. He'd been reading Galatians, and he came across the verse that said, "Bear ye one another's burdens, and so fulfil the law of Christ." This was what the Amish strove to live—but going to a neighbor with a vulnerability wasn't always easy. It took humility—a painful amount, he realized now. But Rue needed to belong to more than just him—she needed to belong *here*.

The day was sunny, with some fluffy mounds of cloud sailing overhead. The bees seemed extra busy this morning, circling the wildflowers that grew in the ditches lining the road, and he got that old feeling of nostalgia. It had been a long time since Thomas had driven out this way. Two or three years, actually. He'd been avoiding it ever since he got back from his extended Rumspringa. It held memories that he no longer knew how to process.

Thomas glanced down a familiar side road that led to a creek he and Noah used to play in as boys. It wasn't deep enough to swim, but it had been wet enough to play in on a hot summer day after chores.

"I used to live down here," Thomas said.

"Really?" Patience shot him a curious look.

"You see that house up ahead—the one with the trees in front?" It had been whitewashed when they lived there, but it was the same house. "That was ours."

He and his brother helped their *daet* whitewash the house and the chicken coop every few years. The winter wind had a way of blasting the paint, and they liked to keep their home looking bright and fresh. Daet worked as a farmhand at a local dairy, and Mamm had kept house, like the other Amish women did.

"You really had no idea they weren't born Amish?" Patience asked, switching to German.

Thomas shrugged. "I had no idea. You tend to think your home is normal… Looking back on it, I suppose there were a few signs. My parents spoke English when they were alone. I used to think it was their way of hiding what they were saying from us kids. And maybe it was. Sort of like we're doing now to keep Rue from understanding us… But now, I realize, it was more than that, because the only time they could have talked freely in their first language would have been when they were alone together."

How unsettling was this for Patience to hear about? He'd worked through a lot of his own anger about his parents' secrets over the last few years, but there were still times when his feelings about it took him by surprise. When his father died and his mother left the community, he'd lost both parents and his sense of place within his own community all at once. He'd been bereft and adrift. He'd needed every ounce of charity that had been offered to him—including the home that Amos and his grandmother opened up for them to live in.

As they came closer to the drive that led up to his childhood home, Thomas noticed some signs of a new family living there—a truck in the driveway, the growl of a tractor coming from farther back on the property. There was a tree closer to the road with low, spreading branches, and a swing still hung from the straightest of them. The rope was new, though. There must be kids living here.

Thomas reined in the horses.

"I used to swing on that swing when I was a little kid like you, Rue," Thomas said, pointing.

"Can I swing on it?" Rue asked.

"No, it isn't ours anymore," Thomas replied.

The door opened and a woman in shorts appeared on the step. She shaded her eyes to look at them, then waved. Rue waved exuberantly back.

"Hello!" Rue shouted.

"Rue, stop that," Patience said briskly, and she exchanged a look with Thomas.

"Hya." Thomas flicked the reins.

"We could ask if I can swing!" Rue said, leaning around Patience to get a better look at the Englisher woman. "She'd probably let me!"

There was no doubt that the woman would let Rue swing, but the price for that would be conversation, and Thomas knew better than to get chatty with the Englishers. Friendships were a two-way street, and for better or for worse, the Englishers in these parts were bent on developing friendships—sharing their experiences, asking too-personal questions.

"Rue, we are Amish," Thomas said. "We keep to ourselves."

"But I'm not," Rue said.

"You're my little girl, so yes, you are," he countered.

Rue frowned at this and leaned back against the seat.

"Her people *are* Englishers," Patience said in German.

"Not anymore," Thomas replied. "I'm raising her Amish. And that's that."

"Of course, but she can't deny her own *mamm*," Patience replied. "Everything she knows and remembers…"

"So I should let her play with Englisher *kinner*, then?" he asked, shaking his head. "I should let her chat with Englisher neighbors? What would you have me do?"

There was a beat of silence, and then Patience said, "I don't know. But her situation might be more complicated than a child born here. That's all I'm saying."

And maybe Patience was right, but what was he supposed to do? Tina had kept him away, and now that Rue was under his care, he had to do what he felt was right. And an Amish life was right. So maybe, in a way, he was doing the exact thing that Tina had done…

"What would you have me do?" Thomas asked, shaking his head. "Her *mamm* was Englisher. Well, so is mine. Am I less Amish because of my parents?"

"I didn't mean that," Patience replied.

"There has to be something said for the life you were raised to, whether or not your parents were raised in the same way," he said, "I'm going to raise her Amish—and there will be no chatting with Englisher neighbors. She'll be Amish through and through by the time she's old enough for her Rumspringa."

And if God blessed his efforts, then she'd stay Amish, too.

"You're her *daet*," Patience said simply.

"I know what it's like to have connections…out there," he said.

"Then you understand how she feels, I imagine," Patience said.

"I understand what she *needs*," he replied. "And she needs to find her place in our community. She needs the stability, the sense of who she is on the narrow path. She doesn't need distraction or reminders of the life she came from. She needs a solid future."

He was frustrated, and he attempted to relax his iron grip on the reins. This child was so determined to cling to her Englisher upbringing, and while he couldn't entirely blame her, he didn't know what to do. There was no halfway with the Amish life.

"Thomas…" Patience said.

He looked over and she reached past Rue and put a hand on his upper arm. Her touch was warm and gentle, melting away the irritation rising up inside him.

"Yah?" he said.

"You're a good *daet*." She smiled then, and he sucked in a slow breath.

Amish families were calm and collected. Already, he was feeling himself getting riled up at the thought of everything he could not control, but at a touch from her hand, he was reminded of everything he was supposed to be. It made him want to close his fingers around hers, tug her closer against him… But there was a child between them, and this new addition to his life had to have his focus.

A man could make a good many mistakes in his life and manage to forgive himself, but the errors in judgment he made with his own *kinner* were the ones that haunted him. He couldn't afford to mess this up with Rue.

They carried on for another couple of miles, then turned down a gravel road that led to the Smoker farm. Patience was silent, and Rue, who hadn't understood any of their German conversation, swung her legs and watched the scenery go by.

As they turned into the Smoker drive, Rue leaned forward when she saw two little girls in the garden. They were barefoot, and they each had plastic ice cream pails that they were filling with weeds. The girls stood up when they saw the buggy and wiped their dirty hands on their dresses.

"There are kids here!" Rue said with a smile.

"*Yah*, you'll have some girls to play with for a little while," Thomas said, and he was glad to see that his daughter was simply happy to see other children, instead of judging whether they were Englisher or Amish.

"This is better than a swing," Rue announced.

Thomas looked over and met Patience's eye. She shot him a smile. Then the door opened and Susan Smoker came out with a wave and a smile. Thomas pulled up the horses.

"Good morning, Susan," Thomas called. "I've come to help Ben with the gate."

"*Yah, yah,*" Susan said. "He'll be glad of that. I think he's in the main barn right now."

"I've brought the new schoolteacher," Thomas said. "Meet Patience Flaud. She'll be teaching some of your girls this year."

"Pleasure to meet you." Susan's smile spread. "Well, come on down and let's get some pie, then."

It was then that Susan's gaze fell on Rue, and Thomas could see the question forming on her face before she said anything.

"This is my daughter, Rue," Thomas said, and he cleared his throat. "It's a long story, but suffice it to say, she's from my Rumspringa. I know I did wrong, and Gott has forgiven me, but... Her *mamm* passed, and she's mine to raise now."

"Oh..." Susan nodded twice. "So she's Englisher, is she?"

"*Yah,*" he admitted.

"She looks it," Susan replied.

Rue, not understanding the conversation, just stared, her blue eyes wide and uncertain. After Thomas hopped down from the buggy, he lifted his daughter down, and then held a hand out to help Patience to the ground, as well. It felt oddly comfortable to have a little girl and a woman in his care today.

But when he turned back to Susan, her easy smile was gone and she was staring at Rue solemnly. The girls arrived from the garden just then, and an older girl opened the screen, a toddler on her hip. The girls were all in matching dresses—some dirtier than others—and he couldn't help but feel a bit of relief. This was the kind of family that Rue needed to see—respectable, well behaved, pious. Except Susan looked a little less welcoming now.

"I hope it's a convenient time for us to get to know each other," Patience said, seeming to read Susan's altered expression at the same time.

"*Yah*, of course," Susan said. "Do you need clothes and shoes for her, Thomas? Because we have some dresses the girls have outgrown and a couple of pairs of shoes, too—"

"*Yah*, thank you," he replied. "That would be a great help. We're starting from scratch, and this was a bit of a shock."

Rue looked up at Thomas uncertainly, and a part of him wished he could stay with her, help her feel more comfortable. But he was here to help Ben, and Patience could help her navigate. Patience seemed to sympathize with Rue's plight, at the very least.

"Go on inside with the women, Rue," Thomas said. "You'll have friends to play with."

It would be all right. This was where his daughter belonged—with Amish playmates and a community that would help her get a proper start...just as soon as they forgave her father for the mistakes that had brought her into the world.

Patience took Rue's hand and followed Susan Smoker into the little farmhouse. Susan looked over her shoulder again at Thomas, who was leading the horses toward the stable, then she sighed. Patience looked in the same direction, watching Thomas's form as he walked away. He was a strong man, but right now, Patience sensed he was at his most vulnerable. It was all coming back on him—his mistakes, his family's problems... To simply look at him, a woman would never know. If Patience had met him under any other circumstances, he'd be just a handsome Amish man, laughter twinkling in his eyes and good looks that could sway just about any single woman.

"It's good to meet you... Patience, is it?" Susan said, drawing Patience's attention back.

"Yes," she said with a smile. "Likewise."

The kitchen was neat, and the table had some basic school worksheets laid out—some printing, some counting... Someone was getting ready for school. The older girl stood by the door with the baby on her hip, looking at Patience shyly. Patience smiled at her, then turned to Susan.

"How many of your girls will be in school this year?" Patience asked.

Rue leaned against Patience's side, and she smoothed a hand over the girl's head.

"Three," Susan replied. "This here is Bethany—she's in seventh grade this year. She's got baby Leora. And Rose is in the fourth grade. Dinah is just starting grade one."

Dinah and Rose were the girls who had been weeding, and Dinah, the smaller of the two, wiped a stray tendril of auburn hair away from her face, leaving a streak of dirt behind.

"And let me see…" Susan turned to spy her fifth daughter munching on a muffin by the counter. "That is our little Ellen. She's only five, so she starts school next year."

Patience smiled at the girls. "I'm glad to meet you. This is Rue. She's four."

"Bethany, let me take the baby," Susan said. "And you take Rue upstairs. Get those dresses from the back of the closet—the ones Dinah outgrew…"

Susan set about giving instructions to her girls, and Bethany took Rue's hand and led her upstairs. The other girls followed, chattering away to Rue in German. Rue wouldn't understand, but they'd figure that out eventually.

"Could you hold the baby for me?" Susan asked. "I'm going to get us some pie."

Patience took the chubby baby girl with a smile, and overhead was the sound of laughter and giggling.

"Now that the *kinner* are out of the way, who is this little girl—Rue, you call her?" Susan asked.

Patience pulled out a kitchen chair and sat down, settling the baby on her lap. "He's Thomas's daughter, as he said. You'd know Thomas's family better than I do—"

"His *mamm*—Rachel—she left us," Susan said. "We know that, but she always was a little different. I'd heard that they'd converted in another community, then moved here. But you could tell—there was just something about them... They spoke English too well, for one. And their German was terrible. After Rachel left, Thomas left, too, for a while, then came back and got baptized. We had no idea there was an Englisher child."

"Yes, well..." It wasn't Patience's place to talk about anything that personal. "She's a sweet little girl. Her *mamm* died in a car accident, and she's doing her best. But she's a fish out of water out here. She's still adjusting to our ways."

Susan nodded sympathetically. "I'm sure she is. But she doesn't speak German?"

"No," Patience replied. "Not a word. Yet, at least. I'm sure her *daet* will teach her."

"And she's...wild and willful?" Susan pressed.

Patience knew what Susan was getting at. It was how they all seemed to see the Englisher *kinner*. And while Rue was Patience's first Englisher child to get to know, she could already see that their assumptions weren't completely true, either.

"She's a little girl with a broken heart," Patience said simply.

"*Yah*, of course." Susan came to the table with two plates of shoofly pie. "I'm just…surprised by all of it. It's a lot to take in. So… What about you, then? Where do you come from?"

"Beaufort," Patience replied.

"And single, it seems?" Susan raised her eyebrows.

Patience laughed at that. "*Yah*. Very single."

"We'll see what we can do about that…" She took her baby back into her lap, then pressed a kiss against her head.

It wouldn't be any use setting her up, though. It wasn't that men her age weren't interested in her upon first sight, but she couldn't offer the family an Amish man yearned for. She wouldn't explain this to Susan Smoker, though. The woman meant well, but Patience would have to find another way to live her life…focus on the ways she could contribute to her community. Teaching school was a valid option.

"Mamm!" Dinah appeared at the top of the stairs. "This girl only speaks English!"

"*Yah,*" Susan replied. "I know. See what clothes fit her, all the same."

"And she wants to know where our TV is!" Dinah added.

Patience felt her own cheeks heat at that. "She's still adjusting to our ways. She needs some time."

"And some scripture, it would seem," Susan said. "Was she raised believing in Gott?"

"I'm not sure," Patience admitted.

"And she says—" Dinah started.

"Enough, Dinah!" Susan said. "Find her clothes, then come back down."

"Yes, Mamm." Dinah disappeared again.

Susan stared up at the staircase for a moment, then turned back to Patience with a tight smile.

"I hope this doesn't reflect badly on our community as a whole," Susan said. "We're actually a very respectable bunch."

Patience didn't know how to answer that, except, this situation wasn't quite so cut-and-dried. Thomas was going through a lot more struggle than they were giving him credit for—all of which he'd confided in her, and she couldn't break his trust. Thomas had quickly become more than just a neighbor, she realized in a rush. He was truly a friend.

"Thomas thought you'd be a good influence," Patience said, lowering her voice. "He needs support— he needs a way to raise her, and that involves a whole community. He sees your *kinner*, and he wants to do the same for his little girl."

"Either we'll be a good influence, or that child will be a bad one," Susan said bluntly. "One or the other."

Patience fell silent, and the girls came back down the stairs, bare feet slapping against wooden floorboards. Their hair was all wild, all except Bethany's, who carried herself like a small adult already, with three dresses in her arms and a pair of girls' running shoes. Susan brightened at the sight of them.

"That's wonderful. That should get you started, Rue," Susan said in English.

"Daddy will give me my clothes back after I'm good," Rue said.

Susan looked over at Patience questioningly, and Patience felt her heart tug toward the little girl. After she was good… Did that mean she thought she was currently bad?

"Thomas took her Englisher clothes," Patience explained. Thomas had meant well, but he'd been wrong there.

"Not forever!" Rue insisted. "He said he's going to give them back, after I'm good for a bit. So I have to be good."

"I don't think they're coming back," Susan said in German.

Rue's eyes narrowed—seeming to dislike the switch in language.

"You needed shoes," Patience said, turning to Rue. "That's so nice of the girls to share theirs with you."

"I don't fit them anymore," Dinah announced. "They're too small for me."

Rue looked at the shoes doubtfully. "I like pink."

"We wear black shoes in our community," Susan said.

"I like pink," Rue repeated. There it was—her stubborn streak that was so problematic.

"There are pink running shoes?" Dinah asked, switching to English, too.

"No," Bethany replied. "Not for us. That's what the Englishers wear."

"I'm not Amish," Rue said simply. "So I can wear pink shoes."

The girls exchanged looks, but Dinah's gaze was fixed on Rue with a look of open curiosity. Ellen was staring, too. Patience could all but see those little gears running for both girls. They were being exposed to a brand-new idea today—that Englishers had things that sounded downright wonderful to a small girl, like pink shoes.

"Rue, say thank you," Patience said, forcing a smile.

"Thank you," Rue said quietly.

Yes, she could see the problem here, but if that stubborn spirit could be turned to use her strength of resolve in favor of the Amish life, all would be well.

"Come play outside, Rue," Dinah said, holding her hand out to the smaller girl. "I'll show you the chickens."

Rue smiled at that. "We've got a rooster named Toby, and my daddy wants to eat him!"

"Toby will probably be tasty," Ellen said in a matter-of-fact tone, following the other girls as they clattered outside, leaving Bethany in the kitchen with them. She reached for her baby sister, and Susan handed her over with a smile.

"Dinah's very interested in Rue's Englisher stories," Bethany said, her voice low.

"What kinds of stories?" Susan asked sharply.

"Oh, TVs, their toys, princesses…"

"The Englishers don't really have princesses," Patience said. "It's only a game, and a foolish one, at that. Gott made each of us equal, and we ought not to raise ourselves above each other. It's wrong and only leads to unhappiness. An honest wife with a kind husband

and houseful of *kinner* is far happier than a princess in a tower somewhere."

"You're telling the wrong person," Bethany said, casting a too-grown-up gaze onto Patience. "It's Dinah who needs to hear it. And maybe Ellen."

Patience swallowed. Bad ideas could spread just as quickly as that. It was why the Amish *kinner* were kept away from the Englishers—*kinner* were impressionable. Rue was just a little girl, but she was also a child who didn't want to be Amish, even now. And somehow, Patience felt protective of little Rue...

"Bethany, could you go out and keep an eye on them?" Susan asked.

"*Yah*, sure, Mamm," Bethany said, and she headed out the side door, the baby on her hip.

When the door shut behind her, Susan cast Patience a tired smile. "I know she's just a little girl, and I know you have nothing to do with this... In fact, I feel terrible for you that this is your introduction to our community. But we need to be careful with our girls. I'll suss up some more clothes for her for winter—I've got some warm clothes put away in storage that she can have, and some boots, too. But I can't have her back here to play with my girls."

Patience met the woman's gaze. "She's very young..."

"So are mine."

Patience nodded.

"Look, I'm sorry to put you in the middle of this," Susan said with a shake of her head. "My husband can tell Thomas himself. I just thought I should mention it, all the same."

Patience looked toward the window where she could see the girls out by a white-painted chicken coop beside which the chickens ran free. Rue had squatted down to be closer to the hens that were pecking at the ground, and Ellen and Dinah stood close by. There was a peal of laughter and Rue looked up, her eyes glittering with delight.

"You haven't started your pie," Susan said. "And Patience, you make sure you come back to see me, yourself. It'll be so fun to have another woman around to chat with…"

But Patience wasn't listening. Rue would never be Amish enough, Patience realized, her heart sinking. She'd always be the girl with the Englisher *mamm*, and there'd be no changing people's knee-jerk reaction to that fact. They had families of their own to protect, *kinner* they longed to shelter, and Rue was a walking, breathing threat to their careful plans. This was going to break Thomas's heart.

Chapter Seven

They all left after Thomas was finished helping Ben Smoker with his gate. As the horses made their way back home without much guidance from Thomas, Rue chattered excitedly about her new friends, which only made Patience feel worse for the poor thing. Even Thomas seemed cheerier after the visit—apparently, Ben hadn't had the chance to fill him in on his wife's request that Rue stay away from the Smoker girls. When they got back to the house, Mary needed help with the laundry, and Thomas went to work at the carpentry shop, leaving the women to their own work. There was no chance to talk to Thomas alone, not without drawing undue attention to herself, so she needed to wait until the men returned that evening and it was time for her to head back to the Kauffmans' house.

By dinnertime, a clothesline of laundry fluttered outside—and this time, there were men's shirts and pants, two of Mammi's dresses and two tiny dresses lined up next to all the adult clothing.

The men came inside smelling of wood shavings and hard work. Amos was telling a story that made Noah laugh, but Thomas remained silent, his gaze immediately seeking out Patience in the kitchen. There was something about the spontaneity of his attention that warmed her cheeks. Rue spotted her father and gave him a shy smile.

"I have something different for you today," Thomas said, squatting down. He had something wrapped in a handkerchief, and Patience paused to watch.

"What is it?" Rue asked, coming closer. She pulled aside the cloth and her eyes lit up.

"It's a rooster!" Rue exclaimed, holding it up. "It's a Toby, Daddy!"

Patience got a glimpse of the gift—a little carved rooster about the size of a tin of tuna. Rue hugged it to her chest, then she sidled up closer to her father and tipped her head onto his shoulder. Thomas patted her head tenderly, then rose to his feet again.

"Did you want to stay for dinner?" Thomas asked Patience.

"Thank you, but I won't stay tonight," she said.

Amos and Noah had turned their attention to nabbing a bun each from the dish Mary had been guarding.

"Would you like to...walk with me back?" Patience asked hesitantly. It was forward of her—far too forward, actually. They were both single, and this would look an awful lot like courting. But she needed to speak to him alone, and she wasn't sure how else to do it.

"Uh—" Thomas's gaze looked uncertain for a moment, and then a smile tickled his lips. "*Yah*, I'd like that."

After saying goodbye, Patience hurried to the door. How this must look! When she got outside, her face felt like it was blazing, and when she glanced over at Thomas, she found him looking mildly amused.

"This looks terrible," she burst out. "I'm not really this forward."

"I didn't think you were," he said.

"I'm not trying to start something, Thomas," she added.

"That's too bad," he replied, his warm gaze catching hers. He was teasing—she could see it in the glint in his eye.

They started their walk down the drive, but Thomas didn't seem in a big hurry. He sauntered along slowly enough.

"I just had to talk to you alone, and I didn't want to draw any attention to it because Rue has been through enough lately, and—" Patience looked back over her shoulder and Thomas did the same. Mary was looking out the door after them, and when she was spotted, she whisked back inside.

"I don't think it worked," Thomas chuckled. "What's going on?"

"It's Susan Smoker," Patience replied. "Did Ben say anything to you?"

"No." He sobered now. "What's the problem?"

Patience licked her lips. "Oh... Well, it seems that Susan—" She didn't want to have to say this out loud. It was cruel, and when she turned to look at Thomas again, he reached out and caught her hand. It wasn't a casual touch, either—it was purposeful, steadying.

"Patience, what is it?" He kept her fingers clasped in his, and there was something about his warm, strong grip—she couldn't let herself appreciate it. So she tugged her hand free. Thomas seemed to realize what he'd done then, too, and he pulled his hand back to his side.

"She says that Rue can't come back," Patience said. "I'm sorry. I tried to point out that her daughters could be a good influence for Rue, but…"

Thomas was silent for a moment, and Patience could see the emotions clashing over his face—anger, frustration, hurt. These were people Thomas thought he could trust to help him in his most vulnerable time as a brand-new *daet*. He'd been wrong.

"Did Rue do something bad?" Thomas asked.

"No! She was fine. She…just talked. As *kinner* do."

"About Englisher things," Thomas surmised.

"*Yah*, about Englisher things."

Thomas sighed, and he started walking again, and she fell in at his side.

"I'm sorry," Patience added. "I don't think Susan is being fair to her."

"I don't think Susan is thinking about Rue at all," he replied quietly. "She's thinking about her own girls."

"That's true…" Patience rubbed her hands over her arms. "Do you want my advice, for whatever it's worth?"

"*Yah*, I do." Thomas looked down at her. "What do you think?"

"Maybe it's better to start out with time alone with you," Patience replied. "It's her relationship to her *daet* that will be most meaningful. Maybe until people relax a little more, you could do some special things with Rue alone."

Thomas chewed the side of his cheek, and they reached the top of the drive. He walked over a few paces until he was shrouded from view at the house by some lilac bushes, the blooms wafting fragrance. He smiled faintly.

Patience went over to where he stood and looked past his shoulder. Anyone in the house could no longer watch them—was that on purpose? They had some privacy—for a moment or two, at least.

"You know how this looks, Thomas," she said.

"They can't see us," he said.

"You know what I mean!" she laughed. "And I know it's my own fault, but I'd really rather not start rumors right away. You should go back."

"I don't want to go back," he replied, and he caught her gaze with a challenge in his eye. "Do you?"

She didn't, actually. It felt nice to stand here in the cool shade of the lilac bushes, this handsome, kind man inches away from her… This was the very thing she couldn't be getting used to, or playing with.

"I'm your first friend here," he said. "And I will make sure to set everyone straight as soon as I get back to the house."

"Do you promise?" she asked quietly.

"*Yah.* I promise. Besides, we haven't figured out what I'll do with Rue all by myself."

Patience was silent for a moment, her mind going back to her own childhood. "My *daet* used to take me and my sisters to the river. We had one that ran through our property, and we'd pack up a picnic lunch, and he'd take us out to the river to eat it together. Once, when my *mamm* and sisters had gone to a quilting circle, my *daet* took me to the river alone, and we sat and threw stones into the water…"

She smiled at the memory. Her *daet* had been a loving man, and he had a way of making every single one of them feel like the favorite.

"There's a creek I used to play in as a boy," Thomas said. "My brother and I used to go there together after chores were done, and we'd dam it up with stones, and then let the water through again in a rush… I pointed it out on the way to the Smokers' place."

"That's right. I remember. A creek is part of a complete childhood," she said.

"I don't know if Rue would even want that much time alone with me," Thomas said. "I'm the gruff one—the one who punishes."

"Rue loves the rooster," Patience countered.

"Yah." He smiled. "I got that one right." He paused, the sound of birds twittering filling the silence as his gaze moved slowly over her face. "Would you…come with us?"

Did she dare? It wasn't that she didn't want to, it was that she might want this time with Thomas and Rue a little too much. She didn't belong here—not like that.

"I'm not sure I should," she admitted.

Thomas nodded. "Okay. I understand. I'm sorry if

I'm crossing lines I shouldn't. I know you'll find some nice man sooner or later and he'll marry you, but—"

"It isn't that," Patience said, shaking her head. There wouldn't be other men. She knew that already. "I don't want to intrude. You don't have to entertain me or anything. And this is about you and Rue. I'm…an outsider."

"No more than I am," he said with a sigh.

A bug fluttered next to her face and Thomas reached out and brushed it away. The movement was impulsive, but once his hand was next to her face, he didn't pull back, and neither did she. He touched her cheek with the back of one finger, and that warm gaze met hers. She felt goose bumps rise on her arms, but she didn't drop her gaze. His eyes moved down to her lips, and he stepped closer.

"She's comfortable with you," he murmured.

Patience meant to answer him somehow, but there were no words in her head, and all she seemed able to feel was the warmth of his chest emanating against her and the tickle of his breath against her face. The moment seemed to deepen around them—even the sound of the birds seeming to drift away. She swayed toward him, and he caught her hand in his, stepping closer, too. But the growl of a car engine was too much to ignore, and they both took a step back as a car swept past them, a whoosh of air ruffling her dress around her legs.

She let out a shaky sigh, suddenly feeling very alone on that street with the gulf between them. What had just happened there? If it weren't for the car, would he have kissed her? She dropped her gaze.

"Thomas—"

"Patience, I—"

They both started talking at once, then they both halted. Patience looked up at him again, some heat in her cheeks.

"I'd like it if you came along for our picnic to the creek. That's all," Thomas said, clearing his throat.

That was all... And maybe whatever had just happened in that moment was just in her imagination.

How could Patience say no to going with Thomas and Rue to the creek? Because she wanted to go along, too, and somehow some time with this man, even if it was nothing more than friendship, felt like a chance at some fleeting happiness. She smiled hesitantly.

"Okay," she said.

"Yah?" A smile turned up his lips. "The shop is closed tomorrow, so... It's a day off anyway. Come over after breakfast, and we'll head out to that creek I used to know."

"Are you sure you wouldn't rather bring your brother?" she asked. He shared the memories with Thomas, after all.

"Nah." A playful grin came back to his face. "I think I prefer you."

Was that flirting? She rolled her eyes. "You could bring the whole family."

"I could." Was that confirmation that he would? He didn't say anything else, but he smiled again teasingly. "Will I see you?"

"Yah." Patience nodded. "I'll see you then."

Patience paused, then turned and took a few steps toward the Kauffman property.

"Are you flirting with me, Thomas?" she asked, turning.

Thomas turned back and hooked his thumbs into the front of his pants. "What if I were?"

"I'm not a good one to flirt with, you know," she said.

"Then don't worry about it," he replied, but that teasing glint hadn't left his eye, either.

Patience didn't have an answer for that, so she hid her smile by turning around and continuing down the road. When she glanced over her shoulder, Thomas was heading back to his drive.

And what if a man flirted a little? It was nice to be noticed and appreciated. It didn't have to go any further than that. She'd just have to be careful not to let things go too far. And she could do that—she knew where things stood. She was helping a man bond with his little girl, and that was a good thing.

Rue needed all the bonding she could get.

As Thomas walked back down the drive toward the house, his mind was spinning. He hadn't intended to flirt—he knew better than that. Amish courted—they thoughtfully and purposefully moved toward a marital union. They didn't flirt and fool around. But there was something about Patience that sparked the competitive male inside him, and the ability to make her blush or smile just like that... But he wasn't looking for romance right now. He was trying to find his balance being a *daet*, so trying to make her smile—it was inappropriate.

But there was something about her—something that tugged at him in spite of all the reasons he should be keeping his distance. And he'd almost kissed her. That realization in itself was a surprise, because he hadn't been thinking of that when he asked her to step behind the lilacs on the street. He'd only been thinking of Mammi, who was likely standing at the front window, watching hopefully for some sign of blooming romance. And knowing Amos, he wouldn't have been far behind.

But that instinct to flirt, to draw her eye—that came from a different source. And the last time he'd listened to it, he'd found himself in a relationship with Tina. His instincts led him wrong, and he needed Gott's guidance if he was going to be the kind of man his daughter could be proud of.

When he got back to the house, the food was on the table—roast beef and mashed potatoes. It smelled wonderful and his stomach rumbled in response to it. Everyone had started eating. They looked up as Thomas came back inside, and he caught Noah's knowing glance.

"Sorry about that," Thomas said, and he slid into his place next to his daughter. She had the carved rooster sitting next to her plate. He smiled down at Rue as she plunged her fork into a fluffy pile of mashed potatoes, topped with a pool of gravy.

"So you saw her off, did you?" Amos said in German. He passed a platter of beef down the table toward Thomas.

"Yah," Thomas said, accepted the platter and served himself two slices.

"She's very pretty," Mary added. She didn't look up from her plate, though. She took a bite of meat and chewed deliberately slowly.

Thomas chuckled. "I know what you're doing."

"Us?" Mary said innocently. "She's a lovely woman. We're just...pointing it out."

"And single," Amos added with a grin. "We've all confirmed that."

"She also seems to like you—which is a point in her favor, because look at you," Noah joked.

Thomas laughed, and shook his head. "It isn't what you think."

"What are they talking about?" Rue asked, leaning closer.

"They're teasing me," Thomas replied. "They think Patience is pretty, and that I should take more notice of it."

Rue frowned slightly. "Oh."

Thomas shook his head. "Someone pass me the potatoes, please."

But despite his protest to the contrary, he was noticing her. She was beautiful, but even so, in their friendship, he sensed that she was holding back in that regard. Was it the man she'd left behind who still filled her heart? And was that all this was—some petty jealousy over a man he'd never even met? Some male competition? Because that would be disappointing.

"Can I go back to see the girls again?" Rue asked.

"No," Thomas said softly.

Noah looked up when he said that. "Why not?"

"It's nothing," Thomas said quickly. "I have something else for Rue and me to do tomorrow. We're going on a picnic."

Mary smiled at that. "Good! That sounds fun."

"Just the two of you?" Amos asked.

"Patience is going to come along," Thomas replied, and he knew how this looked, so he added, "If you all want to come, that would be...very nice."

Amos shook his head, his mouth full, and Noah chuckled.

"Nah," Noah said. "I've got some things to work on here at home."

"And I have some sewing of my own to do, dear," Mary said. "I couldn't possibly."

They were making it so that he'd get time alone with Patience, and he knew it. But at least he'd invited them, even if he was relieved they'd turned him down flat.

"It will be fun, Rue," Thomas said. "I'll take you to a creek I used to play at when I was a boy. You can play in the water and look for tadpoles. We'll pack a lunch to take along."

Rue smiled up at him, and he felt a well of love for his little girl. Some time together—Patience was probably right. What Rue needed was her *daet*, not a bunch of strangers. She needed family, and if there were to be *kinner* in her life, maybe they ought to be siblings.

Chapter Eight

Saturday morning, Thomas, Noah and Amos went out to do their morning chores—mucking out the stable, bringing hay for the horses, cleaning the chicken coop and gathering eggs. Rue came with them wearing her new-to-her running shoes instead of her pink flip-flops, and she stood to the side obediently when they told her to. There was no wiggling or laughter. She was utterly serious, watching everything they did.

"Are you trying to learn how to do the chores, little one?" Amos asked her with a smile.

"I'm being good," she replied seriously. "And I'm not getting in the way."

"Come carry the egg bucket," Noah said.

She looked askance at Thomas first.

"Sure," he chuckled. "Why not? But don't hug Toby."

"I won't hug him," Rue replied. "Not even once."

The men chuckled to themselves and carried on with their chores. Thomas was rather impressed with Rue's improved behavior. Was that because she'd seen some

Amish girls who knew what was expected of them? While there wouldn't be more visits with the Smokers, maybe that one visit had been enough. Maybe his fatherly instinct had been right, and he felt a wave of gratefulness for one small step that had seemed to work in his favor, after all. Gott surely did work in mysterious ways, and maybe this was one of them.

When they got back to the house, Amos and Noah sat down with some hot coffee and Mary went off into the sitting room with her Bible. Thomas set about packing their picnic lunch and Rue waited until Thomas was nearly finished before she tugged at his pants.

"Yes, Rue?" he said.

"Was I good?" she asked.

"*Yah*, very good," he said. "Get me three napkins out of that drawer there." He pointed with his socked toe.

Rue opened the drawer and pulled out three cloth napkins, and he tossed them on top of the food and then closed the basket up. It would be a tasty lunch—roast beef sandwiches, pie, apples, some slices of cheese and a bottle of apple juice.

"Have I been very good?" she asked, and she fixed him with a direct stare.

"*Yah...*" For such a small girl, she was filled with a strange intensity.

"Can I have my clothes back, then?" Rue asked, her voice shaking just a little.

"Your clothes." Her connection to the Englisher world—the clothes all the adults knew had to go. He'd been hoping she'd forget, quite honestly, that after she settled in she wouldn't even think of her Englisher clothes again and he could quietly dispose of them.

"Yes. I need them. They're mine." Her eyes welled with tears, but she didn't cry, and she didn't look down. She stared up at him hopefully. He looked at Amos and Noah. They'd overheard Rue's request and they stared back at him in silence, offering no hint into what they were thinking.

"Well…" He swallowed. "You can't wear them, Rue. You know that, right?"

She didn't answer, but her lip trembled. Her face was so pale, but those eyes were filled with a determined fire.

"They aren't Amish," he added gently.

"They're *mine*," she whispered hoarsely, and the intensity of her gaze nearly choked him.

Thomas had a choice here—keep the clothes, and possibly destroy them, or give them back. She was only a child and didn't know what was best for her life yet. And he was her father—it was his job to guide her, whether it made her happy in the moment or not. But that little suitcase of Englisher clothes… He knew what they meant to her, and even if he wanted to erase her Englisher side, it wouldn't be possible anyway. Nor did he have the right to do it. She'd come into this world because of his relationship with her Englisher mother. And now he was trying to undo it?

"Rue, I'm going to promise you something," Thomas said quietly.

"Okay?" Rue said hopefully.

"I am not going to do anything to your clothes.

They're safe in my closet right now, and I won't hurt them or get rid of them. They're still yours, okay?"

Maybe that would be enough and given time she'd finally forget about them. Maybe she'd see that the Amish life he offered her was worth more than a suitcase of purple and pink summer wear.

"Can I have them back *now*?" Rue pressed earnestly. Her hands were balled up into fists at her side. "I was *good*. I'm a good girl. Can I have them?"

The "no" was on the tip of his tongue, and he almost said it, but he couldn't bring himself to. She wanted those clothes so desperately, her whole body trembling with her desire to have them back, and he couldn't be the one to keep them from her.

"Of course you're a good girl," he said tenderly.

She stared at him, mute, and her eyes filled with hopeful agony. He was beaten. He knew it, and when he looked over, Amos and Noah had both dropped their gazes into their coffee cups. They knew it, too, apparently.

"Yes," he said, at last. "You can have them back. But you can't wear them."

"Okay…" Rue visibly deflated with relief, and the tears that had welled up in her eyes finally rolled down her cheeks. "Thank you, Daddy."

"Oh, Rue," he said softly, and he squatted down next to her and gathered her into his arms. She leaned her face into his shirt and her tears soaked into it, wetting his chest beneath. She cried softly with big, shuddering sobs. Had she been carrying that around inside her all this time? Had he been too harsh on her? He rose to his feet, picking up Rue in his arms as he stood. "I'll give them to you now."

He went up the stairs, his daughter in his arms, and he carried her into his bedroom. His bed was neatly made, the floor swept, and his window open just enough to let a breeze inside. He set Rue on the edge of his bed and went to his closet and pulled out the little suitcase.

Rue jumped down and gathered it up in her small arms.

"Oh, thank you!" she breathed. "I love my clothes, Daddy. I do! I really love them."

And he knew it wasn't about her clothes so much as her mother. She loved her mother most desperately, and this was her last link to the mother she'd likely forget over the years. She wouldn't retain many of her memories of Tina, and he was sorry for that.

"All right, then," he said, a lump in his throat. "Go put those in your room, and then we'll go down, okay?"

Thomas waited for her at the top of the stairs, and when Rue rejoined him, they headed back down, Rue scampering happily on ahead. There was a knock at the door when he got back into the kitchen, and Amos rose to open it.

As expected, Patience stood on the step, and Thomas felt a wave of relief as she came inside.

"I think we're ready to go now," Thomas said. "Come on, Rue."

"I got my clothes back, Patience!" Rue said as they all headed outside. "Because I was good. I was extra good. I didn't hug anything. Nothing at all!"

Patience laughed and held out her hand for Rue, and

Thomas headed over to the stables to hitch up horses. He felt deflated, exhausted and not entirely sure he'd done the right thing, either with taking her clothes away to begin with, or with giving them back. He'd certainly made an impression on her, but what would she take away from that? That her *daet* was capable of strange cruelty? That she was required to behave perfectly in order to keep what was rightfully hers?

Gott, I don't know how, but I've already gone wrong here. I need Your help.

Within a few minutes, they were in the buggy and headed up the drive to the road.

"So you gave her back the clothes?" Patience asked in German.

"Yah," he replied. "I did. I… It might have been a mistake. I realize that. The elders would tell me so, I'm sure."

"But you're her *daet*. It's your call," Patience replied.

"It is," he said grimly.

"For what it's worth," Patience said, "and this coming from a schoolteacher who's never once taught school, so you can take that into account… I think you did the right thing."

"Yah?" He looked over at her, surprised. "I thought I caved in, actually."

Patience shrugged. "But you didn't break her heart."

Thomas smiled to himself. *Yah*, that was true. How fondly would she think of the Amish life if her Amish *daet* was the one to keep breaking her heart?

"I do have an idea of what you could do with her Englisher clothes," Patience said.

"What's that?" he asked.

"You could make a quilt from them," Patience said. "That way, her clothes would be preserved in an Amish way, and she'd still have those memories of her *mamm* close by."

Thomas nodded. "*Yah.* That's a good idea, actually."

It was a solution that hadn't occurred to him. Maybe it took a woman's touch to get there. He glanced over at Patience and smiled. Did she know how much she did for him, just by being here at his side while he waded through the biggest challenge of his life?

"What's a good idea?" Rue asked.

Had he said that in English? He hadn't meant to, but there was no harm done.

"What if we made a very special quilt—that's a blanket for your bed—out of your old clothes?" Thomas asked. "You see, you're growing fast, and soon you won't be able to even squeeze into those clothes. And in the winter, they'll be too cold. But if you had a quilt, when it's cold, you could wrap yourself up in it."

"Ooh…" Rue smiled. "*Yah*, I like that."

Yah. Had he heard that right? She'd answered like an Amish girl. He looked over Rue's head to find Patience smiling, too, with a twinkle in her eye.

"Good, then," he said, not wanting to draw attention to it. "We'll see what we can do."

The creek was set back from the road a little way, shaded by spreading trees. Patience could feel all tension seeping out of her at the tranquil scene—grass rippling in a warm breeze, lush trees, the babble of water that she couldn't yet see, although she knew the land well enough to know that the line of trees would be along its banks. A swarm of sparrows flapped up like a sheet in the wind farther on down the stream, billowed, then settled again in the trees. Thomas tied up the horses with a long enough line to let them graze, and he carried the basket as well as a worn blanket down toward the water with Rue dancing along ahead of them.

Patience had been thinking about that tender moment between them at the lilac bushes all evening, and she'd prayed earnestly that God would simply take away whatever it was that seemed to be brewing between them. She prayed for God to provide for Thomas and Rue—to give them the *mamm* in their family that they needed. She knew that wouldn't be her, and while the prayer did stick in her throat just a little, she prayed that Thomas's wife would capture his heart and they'd love each other well.

It was the kind of prayer that a good woman prayed—at least, that's what she thought. A good woman should be able to pray a thankful prayer for other people's blessings, but she still found that it hurt to pray it. Maybe it was some selfish, sinful corner of her heart that wished he could stay single, too, and they'd remain close friends, and she wouldn't have to watch him move on with another woman.

But out here by a babbling creek, the wind ruffling her dress and Rue laughing at the sheer freedom of the morning, she had to silently pray for strength. It would be too easy to fall for this man, and there would be no benefit in it. She wasn't the wife for him.

"So you used to play here?" Patience said in English.

"*Yah*. My *mamm* would pack me and Noah a lunch and send us off on her floor-washing days. She always said we got in the way more than we helped, so we'd carry our lunch down here and we'd play for hours until our food was gone and we were good and hungry again. I used to use a rope and put it over a branch and we'd swing over the water."

Patience could almost see them—two sun-browned boys whooping and playing.

"Were there only two of you in the family?" Patience asked. It was a noticeably small family for the Amish.

"*Yah*." Thomas frowned. "I asked my *mamm* if she'd have more babies, and she always said that Gott was the one who gave *kinner*, and that I should take it up with Him. I never got more explanation than that."

Patience could understand that kind of answer. She had a similar one, herself, except she wouldn't have the pleasure of having even one child of her own. She often wondered why Gott had taken away this ability for her. There didn't seem to be any benefit to anyone else by denying her the simple ability to be a *mamm*. She was born Amish, with one duty to a husband, and unable to provide it.

"So you wanted more siblings?" she asked.

"*Yah*, of course," he said. "My friends all had big families and lots of little brothers and sisters to pester them, and I felt like I missed out a bit. I had Noah, but our home was a quiet one. I liked the mayhem."

"I suppose you could make up for that with a houseful of *kinner* of your own," she said, hoping her voice didn't sound strained.

He shot her a grin. "I suppose I could."

Was he imagining those *kinner* belonging to them? Because she was…even though she knew it wasn't a possibility.

"Come on," he said, putting down the basket. "Let's find a spot for the blanket."

Thomas unfolded the worn quilt and handed her one side of it. They shook it open, and then spread it down on the lush grass that lined the water.

"Can I go in?" Rue pleaded. "Can I go into the river?"

It wasn't much of a river, and there hadn't been much rain that spring, either, so it was only a few inches deep and rippled over the rocks in a merry babble.

"*Yah*, go ahead," Thomas said, and he crossed his arms over his chest, watching Rue pull off her shoes and dip her toes into the water.

"It's warm!" Rue said, and she lifted her dress up above her knees and stepped farther in. "Are there fish, Daddy?"

"There might be," he said. "If you look really closely."

Patience couldn't help but smile, and she put the picnic basket on one corner of the blanket, then lowered herself down to sit on it, adjusting her skirt to cover her legs. Thomas settled himself next to her, leaning back on his hands, and she couldn't help but notice the ripple of muscle that was visible in his forearms. She purposefully looked away, and her gaze fell on the initials sewn onto the edge of the quilt—RW.

"Who made this quilt?" she asked.

"My *mamm*. Years ago."

It was a simple block quilt, and she could see a few blocks that hadn't lined up perfectly. It was the kind of quilt a girl started on, learning as she went. Although, Rachel would have been a wife already when she started learning, she realized.

"I made a few quilts like this," Patience said, running her fingers over the stitching. "In fact, a basic block quilt would be best for Rue's quilt, I think."

"Would you be willing to make it for her?" Thomas asked. He looked over at her, and there was something about his warm gaze that made her look down again.

"Sure, *yah*. I could."

"I'd pay you for your time," he said. "I'm not trying to take advantage of your good nature, or anything."

"You don't have to pay me," she said with a faint smile. "It will give me something to work on in the evenings."

It would give her something to do besides grading papers, quite frankly. And it would help her to feel like she was useful, because that was the thing that had been hanging on her these last few years—a feeling of general uselessness. Yes, she could cook and clean, but so could her *mamm*. She was the barren, single daughter left at home—loved, of course, but not really needed for the running of things. Teaching school was supposed to help with that, but now that she was here in Redemption, she wasn't so certain that it would fill all the gaps.

There were a few left over. What Patience wanted most was a home of her own, but that didn't seem likely.

"I messed up by taking Rue's Englisher clothes away," Thomas said.

Patience looked over at him, surprised by the abrupt change in subject. His expression was less guarded now, and he watched his daughter play in the water as he talked.

"I shouldn't have done that," he went on. "If you'd seen her doing her very best to be good—so solemn and careful—and then begging me with tears in her eyes to give them back…"

Patience's heart gave a squeeze. "She's learning, but so are you."

"*Yah*, but I'm the parent, and it's in my power to ruin her. She can't ruin me." Thomas sighed. "If you ever notice I'm doing something that I probably shouldn't, tell me, okay?"

"Are you sure you want me to?" Patience asked. "It would be intruding, interfering."

"It would be insight from a friend," he replied, and he turned his dark gaze toward her.

"Am I a friend?" she asked.

"*Yah*. I thought so. You don't?"

Patience smiled, then shrugged. "I don't know. I'm a neighbor lending a hand. I wasn't sure if you'd want more from me after this."

She knew that her words were loaded—wanting more from her… And she didn't really mean the implied intimacy, because even if he did want more from their relationship, he'd change his mind once he knew that she'd never have *kinner*. She caught Thomas's gaze locked on her, and she looked up, smiling self-consciously.

"What?" she said.

"You're very beautiful," he said quietly.

His words slipped beneath her defenses, and she felt her cheeks heat. Why did he say things like that?

"I'm the plain sister in my family," she said with a low laugh, trying to push away his compliment. "I was never the pretty one. Trust me on that."

"You're the pretty one for me," he replied.

Did he really think so, or was he flirting? It was hard to think of herself in that way.

"You shouldn't talk like that," she said. "I'm the schoolteacher, and you'll be embarrassed later when Rue is in my classroom and you'll remember sweet-talking me by the creek."

"I won't be embarrassed," he said, and his expression was completely honest. "I'm only telling you the truth."

He'd be married to someone else, no doubt, and that would change things. But she didn't want to say that out loud. There was something about this quiet morning that she wanted to protect. Even if he never thought of it again, she would.

"Tell me about you," he said after a moment of silence. "You have sisters, you said."

"There are six of us—and I'm the youngest," Patience replied. "They're all married now with *kinner* of their own. So I'm the favorite aunt of seventeen youngsters."

Thomas chuckled. "I like that."

"One of my nephews has a learning disability, and I

was the one who taught him to read and write," she said. "His name is Mark, and when he was born, he had the cord wrapped around his neck so he didn't get oxygen fast enough. It affected him."

"That's awful," Thomas said.

"Gott brought him through. And now, he's the funniest kid—he tells jokes and has the other kids in stitches. The teacher couldn't take the time with him, though, and I think he distracted the class a lot because he'd rather joke than admit the work was too hard for him. He kept getting notes sent home, and his *daet* was just beside himself trying to get him to behave. But I sat him down and took the time he needed to really understand. And after that, I thought I'd like to teach. It's very satisfying watching *kinner* catch on, especially when they've really struggled with it."

"They must miss you," Thomas said.

"Oh… I suppose. Somewhat. But they all have their own families."

"You're a part of their families," he countered.

"I know. And they do miss me, I'm sure. I'm just feeling the—" She stopped. She was talking too much.

"Feeling what?" he asked.

"I needed this change," she said, and she forced a smile.

"There's a fish!" Rue called from the creek. She stood there, water just past her ankles, looking down at something. "Patience, come look! There's a fish!"

The distraction was well-timed, and Patience pushed herself to her feet. She kicked off her shoes and went barefoot to the bank of the creek, and then stepped into the rippling water. Rue was right—it was warm, and she made her way slowly over the smooth rocks to where Rue stood.

"See?" Rue said, pointing down at a little stick.

"That's not a fish, Rue," Patience chuckled. "That's a piece of stick."

"Oh." Rue straightened and looked around, but just then Patience saw a flash of silver, and then another one.

"Rue, look—" Patience pointed. "There. Do you see that flash? And there. Those are fish."

Rue bent down to look, her dress drifting in the water, but then she shrieked with delight.

"It's fishes, Daddy!" she hollered. "All sorts of them!"

Patience looked up to find Thomas sitting in the same position she'd left him, leaning back on his hands, his legs crossed at the ankles in front of him and his gaze locked on them. It wasn't just Rue he was watching...

She'd better not get used to this. It wouldn't last—it couldn't! And if anyone spotted them, they'd assume they were courting, when they weren't. Once a rumor like that started, it could be very uncomfortable.

"Are you hungry, Rue?" Patience asked.

Maybe it was better to keep things focused on the little girl who had tugged them together in the first place. Because whatever had started to develop between them could only end in someone getting hurt...and she suspected that someone would be her.

Chapter Nine

Thomas opened the picnic basket, and Rue sat on her knees on the blanket, bouncing while she waited for her food. She ate ravenously, much more than he thought a girl that size could consume. But then, when she'd finally eaten her second piece of pie, she seemed to fill up, and she laid herself down on the blanket with a deep sigh.

"Daddy," Rue said quietly. "Do you know any more stories?"

"Yah," he chuckled. "All sorts."

"Tell me a story about when you were little," she said. "Little like me."

"Like you?" he said.

Patience looked over at him with a smile tickling the corners of her lips, and he suddenly felt shy. What kind of story could he tell that would both please his daughter and impress the teacher? That wasn't going to be easy.

"I'm not sure Patience wants to hear stories," he hedged.

"Oh, I do, though," Patience said, breaking into a full smile. "Tell us a story, Daet. We want to hear one."

Daet. The term warmed his heart, and there was something about how Patience said it—with warmth and familiarity. It almost felt like she could be the *mamm* here.

"Okay, you want a story," Thomas said. He frowned to himself, sifting through his memories of childhood antics, punishments he'd received, his brother's tricks and games... "All right, I have one."

"Is it from when you were little like me?" Rue asked.

"I was a little bit bigger than you," he replied. "But I was still a little boy."

Rue fixed him with a direct stare, and then she yawned. "You can start."

Patience seemed to sense Rue growing tired, too, because she reached out and started to stroke the girl's blond hair in a slow, methodical way.

"One spring, when I was a little boy," Thomas began, "my *mamm* got sick with a terrible flu. The flu turned into pneumonia, which meant that she was sick for a few weeks and had to stay inside. So she gave me a very special job to do—I had to plant the garden."

His mind went back to those days, when his *mamm* and *daet* were the center of his world, and he'd never once suspected that they'd ever been anything other than exactly what they were—Amish. Life had been simple back then, and sweet.

"My *mamm* gave me very specific instructions," Thomas said. "I was to plant three rows of carrots, three rows of peas, three rows of cabbage... But it all seemed very tiring. Mamm said I had to put three seeds in a little hole, and then move down a foot, and put three more seeds in a hole, move down another foot… We had a very, very big garden."

Rue's eyes started to drift shut, but she said, "You were helpful."

"*Yah*, I was helpful," Thomas agreed. "At least I intended to be. At first. But when I started planting, it was a very warm day, and I was tired and cranky, and all by myself out there. It was just me and the dirt. I started to get lazy. I started putting more than three seeds in each hole, and I started putting more space between the holes, just trying to finish up faster. And every time I got to a new row, it just seemed like it would take forever to finish up."

Rue's eyes were shut now, and her breath was coming slowly.

"Rue?" he said softly.

There was no reply. She'd fallen asleep. Just as well. He didn't come out well in this story. Maybe he should have chosen a different one.

"So what happened?" Patience asked.

He looked up, then chuckled. "Oh… I did a terrible job of planting, and my parents found that out when it all came up a couple of weeks later. They got some advice from a neighbor about putting some more seeds in between the ones I'd planted too far apart, and I think they were also advised to give me extra chores for a while."

"Did they?" she asked with a small smile.

"*Yah*. They did." He still remembered that punishment, not because it was so painful, but because he'd known that he deeply deserved it. He'd been so ashamed of himself, not helping properly when his *mamm* had been so sick. "But the most important lesson I learned that day was that what you plant will eventually come up, in life as well as in gardens."

"A good lesson," she said softly.

"*Yah*, a good one." He looked down at his daughter asleep on the blanket. "I made mistakes in my life, Patience, and I am certainly reaping from the mistakes I made, but I can't regret my little girl."

"Sometimes Gott gives us some grace in the middle of our consequences," Patience replied.

And that was what Rue had turned out to be—the most generous gift Gott could have given him, in the form of one little girl whom he hardly deserved.

Rue stirred a little in her sleep, and Thomas pushed himself to his feet, then held out a hand to Patience.

"Let's let her rest," he suggested.

Patience accepted his hand and he tugged her to her feet as well, and as they walked the few yards to the creek bank, he kept her hand in his. Her fingers were soft, and the contact with her felt natural in the moment. He turned to look back at Rue, and Patience leaned into his arm. It was an innocent enough movement, but it reminded him of just how close she was, and he dropped her hand then, and slid his instead around her waist.

She felt good there next to him, his arm around her, her face leaned against his shoulder, and looking down at her, he didn't know why he'd been holding himself back all this time. She was beautiful, insightful, kind…

"Patience," he murmured.

She lifted her cheek from his shoulder and looked up at him, and when her gaze met his, he felt like the rest of the field and trees, the creek and the twitter of birds all seemed to evaporate around him. It was just the two of them—this beautiful woman who had tumbled into his life, and himself. His stomach seemed to hover in the center of him, and he swallowed. She was beautiful, but it was more than that… Looking down at her, he was feeling a tumble of emotion that he couldn't even name. But it felt good, and scary and—he just wanted to be close to her. She met his gaze easily enough, and without thinking better of it, he leaned in, wondering if she'd pull back, but she didn't. Instead, her eyes fluttered shut, and as his lips covered hers, he let out a sigh of relief.

That kiss felt like the culmination of everything he'd been longing for, and when they pulled back and he opened his eyes, he saw Patience staring up at him in surprise.

"Oh…" she breathed.

He couldn't help but grin. "I've been thinking about doing that for a little while now."

"We shouldn't do that," she whispered.

"You didn't want that kiss?" he asked. Because it had felt like she did. If he'd gotten that wrong, he'd feel terrible.

"No, I wanted it," she said, and pink infused her cheeks. She pulled out of his arms. "But we can't."

But why not? They were both single and Amish. They both seemed to be feeling something here—unless she was still uncertain about him because of his family… Or was it her own history?

"Is it the man you left behind?" he asked.

"No…" She shook her head. "Thomas, I'm not the wife for you."

"How do you know?" he asked. Was it his history? His parents? His daughter? Was he not Amish enough for her, after all? All the possibilities tumbled through his head.

"You want marriage and *kinner* and a houseful of life," she said.

"*Yah.* Of course," he said, and he smiled faintly. "Don't you?"

"Thomas, I can't have *kinner.*"

Her words hit him in the stomach, and he frowned slightly, trying to make sense of it. "What?"

"I had surgery that left me…unable to have children. I'll never get pregnant. I'll never have babies of my own."

Thomas licked his lips, this new information clattering through his mind. "Never?"

"Never." Her voice shook. "I don't tend to announce these things, but I should have said something earlier… before this."

"It isn't your fault," he said. "I kissed you. Not the other way around."

"Still, we can't do that again," she said. "You don't just want a family, you *need* one. Rue needs one! And you'll need a woman who can give you that family and fill your house with babies and laughter."

She was right—he did need that family, but it didn't change how he felt when he looked at Patience, or when he thought of her. She'd seeped in through the cracks somehow.

"I can't help how I feel about you," he said at last.

"We should try, though," she replied, and she met his gaze earnestly. "We really need to try."

And somehow, the serious glint in her eye, the pink in her cheeks and her complete intention to shut down whatever this was sparking between them made her even more beautiful to him. Because she wasn't just an attractive woman, she was a good woman…and that appealed to him most of all. Her beauty sank right down to her core.

"Yah," Thomas said nodding. "I'm sorry. I won't kiss you like that again."

She shrugged sadly. "It's no use breaking our hearts over something that will never work, is it?"

"Not really," he agreed.

"You're a good *daet*," she said, and her voice caught in her throat. "You deserve to be a *daet* many times over."

That had been his dream for a long time—a wife and *kinner* of his own. He'd wanted to be ready to be a good *daet*—to mature into it. But the woman he'd have those *kinner* with had stayed a misty blur in his imagination. Suddenly, she seemed to be taking shape—but Patience couldn't be that *mamm* to his *kinner*.

"Have I ruined things between us?" he asked. "By kissing you, I mean. Can we still be friends after that?"

Patience shrugged, but a smile tugged at her lips. "I could forgive it."

Thomas was relieved to hear that, because he didn't want to send her out of his life, either. He wanted her insights, her presence, her advice. And maybe she was right about a romance not working between them, but she was still an exceptional woman.

"Then I'll curb whatever this is I'm feeling," he said.

"Me, too."

Those words made his heart skip a beat, because it meant that she was feeling this, too. It wasn't just him attracted to the wrong woman...

"You, too?" he breathed.

"Yah." She gave him a nod. "But stopping this now is the right thing to do. We both know that."

The right thing was often the hard thing—as an Amish man, he knew that.

"Should we head back, then?" he asked, his voice low.

"Yah. That would probably be smart."

Because staying out here with her by the creek with all this privacy, he wasn't going to be able to back his feelings off quite so easily. She wouldn't know exactly how she made him feel, but he did.

So he headed over to where his daughter was still sleeping on the quilt, and he crouched down, scooping her up in his arms. Her head lolled against his arm, and he felt a rush of paternal love looking into her pale face. He'd never been able to see her as a baby—but he'd wondered about the child Tina had kept from him. He'd missed so much, but he wasn't going to miss anything more.

Rue was his... And she had to be his priority.

"Could you hold her on the ride back?" he asked, rising to his feet.

"Yah, of course," Patience said.

He'd have to be careful, because his feelings for Patience were growing, and if he messed up this fragile friendship with her, he wouldn't be the only one to suffer. Rue did better with Patience in her life, too, and she didn't have many friends who could look past her beginnings and see the bright little girl she was. She needed Patience more than he did—and if friendship was the way to keep her in his daughter's life, then he'd have to protect that friendship with all his might.

His growing feelings would have to be curbed. There was no way around it.

The ride back to the house was a slow one, and the bright sunlight, the tumble of scattered clouds, the buzz of the bees around the wildflowers and the soft, floral-scented breeze weren't enough to soothe Thomas's heart. The ride out to the creek, with his boyhood memories, was so much sweeter than this ride back.

He couldn't help but feel the weight of what he'd done. He should never have kissed Patience. It was wrong, overstepping... And on this side of it, he felt incredibly stupid. Would Patience ever be comfortable with him again? Amish courting was a slow process that involved much conversation before any kisses were exchanged. A man and woman needed to be certain of each other, to truly understand each other. Then there would be no regrets later on if the relationship didn't work out—no lines crossed that would cause any undue embarrassment.

He'd moved too quickly with Tina in the city, too. But that had been pure rebellion—as was his entire time spent with his *mamm* away from Redemption. And it had been loneliness, too, because he'd missed his brother, his friends, the community that had become a part of him. He'd thought that being with his *mamm* would give him the comfort he'd been missing while he was in Redemption, but as it turned out, a *mamm* wasn't enough. He'd needed more than her presence in his life, and he'd reached for a different kind of comfort. He'd known his relationship with Tina was wrong, and he'd done it anyway.

Was he making a similar mistake now—reaching out for comfort where he shouldn't be? Because Patience was a comfort, a definite help, and having her around made an already difficult situation that much sweeter. Was he leaning on her because of his own longing for some compassion and support? Was that even fair?

And maybe on his Rumspringa, his loneliness was just part of growing up when a man realized that "home" was no longer at his *mamm*'s apron. Home started to take on a new meaning, to come with a new sense of urgency to create his own home with his own wife. But Patience had already made it clear that she couldn't be the wife he needed.

Thomas flicked the reins, urging the horses to speed up again. One horse shook its head, making the tack jingle. He was letting his heart lead when he should be praying a whole lot harder. Hearts could go wrong so very easily, and there was no getting around the fact that his heart was definitely entangled with the woman at his side.

Gott, I'm sorry, he silently prayed. *I don't want to go back to old ways. I want to live a pure life that will please You. I don't want to play with this. I want to marry the right woman. Obviously, I was wrong in kissing her, but...*

He looked over at Patience with his daughter cradled in her arms, her cheek resting tenderly against Rue's blond head. Her gaze was on the road ahead, and she seemed to be equally deep in thought.

I'm feeling things for her that will only lead to heartbreak if I let it continue. She's beautiful, and kind, and sweet, and...never to have kinner. *And I know what Rue needs—a family to give her a sense of who she is here in our community.*

Whatever they were feeling for each other didn't matter, because even Patience saw that Rue needed siblings if she was to have a hope of settling into the Amish life on a heart level. He couldn't just raise his daughter for the inevitable heartbreaking day when she left them. If Gott had brought his daughter to him, there had to be a way to raise her so that she'd feel that an Amish life was home. There *had* to be. And Rue's future had to be his top responsibility, not his own comfort.

Take it away, Gott. These confusing feelings that just keep growing—douse them for me. Because I can't seem to get them under control on my own.

The horses knew their way home, and as soon as they got to the drive, they turned in and carried them at an easy pace down the gravel way toward the stables where oats and hay were waiting. Rue woke up and rubbed her eyes. Patience loosened her grip on the girl as she sat upright and looked around herself for a moment in bleary confusion. Then Rue's face fell.

"We left?" Rue asked plaintively.

"We did," Thomas replied, reaching over and giving her leg a pat. "We had to get back."

"Why?"

"Because——" Thomas glanced over at Patience. Because if he'd stayed longer with Patience, it would have made everything harder. He'd have kept feeling this draw toward her, and she'd likely have felt it, too. Leaving had been the right choice—getting back to the bustling distraction of other people.

"Because grown-ups get tired, too," Patience said.

It was a good answer, and he cast her a grateful smile. Thomas reined in the horses, and the side door to the house opened and Amos came outside. He looked almost gray, and he strode up to the buggy, his expression grim. Had something happened? Thomas's first thought was of Mammi.

"Thomas, I'll unhitch the horses," Amos said in German. "You're needed inside."

"What's going on?" Thomas asked.

"Your *mamm* is in there."

Thomas's heart hammered to a stop, and he tightened his grip on the reins, looking toward the house. His *mamm*? She wasn't due for another visit—and when she came, she didn't usually come to the house.

"Did you talk to her?" Thomas asked.

Amos shrugged. "Not much. I mean…pleasantries."

Thomas looked over at Patience, unsure of what to say. Here it was—their family embarrassment.

"You need privacy," Patience said.

He did. He couldn't ask Patience to come help him deal with his mother—this was on him. Rue seemed to sense the tension, even if she didn't understand the language, because her eyes were wide and her little lips were pressed together in a tight line.

"It's okay, Rue," Thomas said. "Come with me. There is someone you'll want to meet."

"Who?" she whispered. "Are they taking me away?"

"No, no," Thomas replied. "No one's taking you anywhere. It's your grandmother."

"Mammi?" Rue sounded confused.

"You have another grandmother." A biological grandmother. A *real* one.

Rue brightened at that, and Thomas got out of the buggy and lifted Rue down beside him. Then he held a hand up to help Patience from the buggy. When she hopped down next to him, he didn't release her fingers right away.

"What do I do?" he whispered.

"You pray," she whispered back.

Thomas licked his lips. He was already praying—a wordless sort of uplifting toward Gott, asking for… He wasn't even sure what. Just wanting to feel Gott there with him—even more of a comfort than this woman beside him. He realized then that he was still holding her hand, and he released her.

"I'll go on back to the Kauffmans', and you'll know where to find me if you need me more today," she said. She made it all sound so rational and simple.

"Yah," he said, his voice thick. "I suppose I'd better go see what she wants."

Patience headed back up the drive, walking briskly, and Thomas looked toward the house. There was no cheery clatter of dishes or the din of laughter. It was ominously silent.

"Come on, Rue," Thomas said, forcing himself to sound cheerier than he felt. "Let's go in."

When Thomas opened the door, Rue went inside ahead of him. She stood in the doorway of the mud-room staring.

"Is that my granddaughter?" Mamm's voice said in perfect, accent-free English. "Hi there, Rue. I'm your grandma."

Thomas followed his daughter into the kitchen, and his *mamm* sat at the kitchen table with a glass of water in front of her, nothing else. She wore her Amish clothes—they looked worn and a little snug. She needed new Amish clothing for her visits, it seemed, but she was still the mother he loved so well—the same laugh lines around her eyes, and her dyed hair had started to grow out a little bit. The last he'd seen his *mamm*, she'd been wearing Englisher jeans and a T-shirt. The memory was strikingly different from the Amish-clad woman before him. Mammi was nowhere to be seen, and Noah sat at the table across from their mother glowering at an empty space on the table.

"Hi, Mamm…" Thomas said.

"Son—" Rachel stood up and circled the table to give him a hug.

"We normally get a coffee in town," he said. "And I thought we were getting together at the end of the month."

"I know," she said. "I just—" She smiled hesitantly. "I want to come back."

Noah's gaze jerked up as she said the words, and Thomas could only assume that his brother was just as surprised as he was.

"What?" Thomas breathed.

"I want to confess and come back to the community," she said, tears welling in her eyes. "I want to come home."

After a decade away, after leaving her sons behind and forging ahead, building a new Englisher life with her sister in the city. After all the things she'd told him—how the Amish life was too controlling, too restrictive, too hard to live… After she'd shown him how the Mennonites could live a life to honor Gott while using all the modern conveniences, too… She'd been so certain. She'd said that their *daet* was the one who wanted to live an Amish life, and she'd been willing to do it with him, but when he died she just couldn't face another canning season.

Thomas shook his head. "I don't understand. Why?"

"And why now?" Noah interjected. "You left us when we needed you most, Mamm. And now that we're grown men, you want to come back?"

Noah's eyes misted, and he looked away again, his jaw set. Rachel sucked in a wavering breath and she looked pleadingly toward Thomas.

"You have Rue now," she said. "You might need my help with her. I can understand where she came from, and the kind of life you want for her. I understand little girls. I could help you in ways that you aren't even considering yet!"

"I want my daughter to stay Amish," Thomas said,

shaking his head. "I don't want her to have more connections with the Englisher world."

Mary came to the top of the staircase, and Thomas stared up at her mutely. She met his gaze for one agonizing moment.

"Rue," Mary called. "Come upstairs with me."

Rue looked at Thomas.

"Go on," Thomas said. "You go with Mammi. This is grown-up business."

"Mammi?" Rachel said softly. She looked like the endearment stung a little—technically, she was Rue's *mammi*, too. Rue walked slowly past Mamm, looking at her in open curiosity as she went by, then headed for the stairs where Mary stood impatiently. The old woman snapped her fingers.

"Rue. Now," Mary said curtly, and Rue picked up her pace as she went up the stairs. When Rue disappeared onto the second floor, Thomas rubbed his hands over his face.

"Did you talk to the bishop yet?" he asked.

"I wanted to talk to you first," she replied. "I'll talk with him afterward."

"You know that's the wrong way to do it," Thomas said. "If you want to come back, you've got to go to him first! You have to talk to the church leadership, confess your wrongdoing, ask to be rebaptized and to be admitted into the community again. This—this is just more flouting of the rules, Mamm!"

"And who taught you those rules?" she snapped. "I did! I raised you to be good Amish men, and I did a good job of it, might I add!"

"So you really want to be Amish again?" Thomas demanded. "After all of it…after you halfway convinced me that this life isn't even what Gott wants of us… Now you think you were wrong?"

"I…" She paused, and then shook her head. "I see things differently now."

They all fell silent and Thomas looked over at his brother. Noah's hands were balled up into fists on the tabletop.

"Are you coming back, then?" Noah asked curtly.

"Do you *want* me to come back, son?" Rachel asked, turning toward her oldest boy.

Noah was silent. He'd never admit it—he was too angry—but Thomas couldn't let this spiral down into anger and emotional punishment.

"*Yah*, we want you to come back," Thomas interjected. "Of course we do."

"Will you…give me a place to live when I do?" Rachel licked her lips, and Thomas could see that was a hard question for her to ask.

"This is Amos's house," Noah said curtly. "And Mary's."

"Mamm, even if I have to find a house of my own, you'll have a place to live," Thomas said.

Tears welled in her eyes. "I miss you both so much… You don't know how much I've missed you. I didn't think I could face an Amish life without your *daet*. He was the one who was most convinced about the theology and all that… But I've had my own Rumspringa, I suppose you could call it. I craved some freedom, to just be my own woman again. I was raised to have a career and an education. I missed theater—operas and plays, especially. I missed that life I used to have… As you know, the Amish life doesn't really allow for all the things that had made me who I was before I got married."

"But do you believe in the church's teachings?" Noah asked dubiously.

"I do. I've gone back to the Bible and looked at the teachings all over again," she said earnestly. "It was having Rue come back to the family that gave me a good mental shake. Tina died so unexpectedly, and I realized that we don't always have the time we think we do."

She wanted to help with Rue, and while he could never turn his own *mamm* away, he couldn't be sure that a *mammi* who'd jumped the fence was the answer for his daughter, either. What he needed most desperately was a deeply devoted Amish wife, and to begin growing the family that would give Rue her roots.

Coming back… Would his mother really do it? Would she come back to the life she found so stifling? Because ten years ago, she'd left this life for the rest of her Englisher family that she'd missed just as desperately. She missed being a "modern woman" with cultured interests and other opportunities. Even if Mamm did come back in earnest, Thomas didn't know how she'd ever find a balance.

Would Rue have any more success than her grandmother?

Chapter Ten

⤬

The next day was service Sunday. It was a more leisurely morning than usual. Samuel went out to tend to the horses and chickens, but the regular work would wait until Monday and the family would get a semblance of a break.

Patience helped Hannah clean up the kitchen after breakfast, and they put some salad fixings aside to bring along for their contribution to the light meal served after worship was done. Last night, Patience and Hannah had baked cinnamon buns, some tarts and oatmeal cookies, and this morning they packed them into tubs to carry with them.

Patience couldn't help but think about Thomas, though. She'd waited to see if he'd ask for her to come back and help with Rue, but he hadn't, and she didn't dare go back. It wasn't her place to insert herself into their family problems, but she was concerned all the same. Thomas had been through more than most men had, and she suspected that his mother's visit was an emotional confusion.

News of Rachel Wiebe's visit had already spread. Samuel saw her waiting for a cab at the end of Thomas's drive, and while he hadn't spoken to her, they had exchanged a silent look.

"Will the Wiebe boys tell the bishop that their mother was here, I wonder?" Hannah said, closing a plastic container. She'd been talking about it all morning.

"I don't know," Patience replied. "Do they need to?"

"She didn't do anything bad enough to get excommunicated from the church, but she's not exactly Amish anymore, either, is she? All after she was baptized."

"*Yah*, there is that…" Patience sighed. "But we're talking about a *mamm* and her *kinner.*"

"A *mamm* who certainly knew better." Hannah didn't look inclined to feel much pity. "There are consequences to everything we do in life, and we need to face them. As does she. I think the bishop should have shunned her— for leaving like she did. Mary Lapp took over with those boys when their *mamm* left—and I know that Mary did her best by them. But Rachel was the one who left them in a difficult position. She was their *mamm*—she owed them better than that!"

"*Yah…*" Patience wasn't adding much to the conversation. She didn't know any more than Hannah did— that Rachel had arrived, Thomas had most certainly seen her, and then…silence.

"Rachel was a good woman," Hannah went on, her voice softening. "I didn't see the tendency to jump the fence in her. She seemed so…proper. But there is no saying how grief will affect some people, I suppose."

"She had a more complicated situation, though," Patience added.

"*Yah*. We found that out too late, didn't we?" Hannah shook her head. "And if we all just abandoned our faith and our *kinner* when we faced loss, what would be the point of even having our community? What is your faith if it crumbles at the point of testing? There are vows we take in marriage, and they are similar to the vows we take at baptism—we vow to be faithful. She broke hers."

"Not in her marriage," Patience qualified. She felt the need to defend Thomas's mother, if she could. She was his *mamm*, after all.

Samuel pulled the buggy up to the side door, and Patience heard the nicker of horses. She'd be attending service this morning with her landlords, but she wasn't sure if she'd even see Thomas today. Would he skip service Sunday? Samuel came inside, and Hannah looked up at her husband with a smile.

"Carry that, would you, Daet?" Hannah said, gesturing to a cloth bag filled with vegetables for salad.

Samuel took the bag, and a stack of treat-filled plastic containers, too. He tramped back out to the buggy, and Patience and Hannah grabbed the last of the food and followed him out.

Service Sunday—the time when everyone gathered together, worshipped Gott as a community and got to see everyone after two weeks. Patience had always looked forward to it, but this Sunday seemed to be a reminder that she needed to keep an emotional distance from

Thomas and Rue. There was no future there for her with the handsome carpenter—and he *needed* a wife.

The services were being held at the bishop's farm, and when they arrived, the buggy field was already nearly filled. A large tent had been erected for the service, and the young men were busy arranging the benches beneath it from the Sunday service wagon. Every Amish community did things in a similar way, but each gathering of a community felt a little different. These were new families with new challenges, and her *mamm* had asked her rather pointedly to keep her eyes open for any single men with *kinner*. Mamm was absolutely convinced that a happy marriage was possible for Patience, and she dearly wished that she shared her mother's optimism there.

After helping Hannah to carry the food to the refrigerated wagon—a community investment that came in handy when keeping food from spoiling during weddings and church services—Patience scanned the unfamiliar faces for a familiar one. She spotted Thomas over by the horse corral in a pair of black pants, a white shirt rolled up to his elbows and his black suspenders and hat. Rue clung to the side of a fence, and Thomas leaned against the top rail, both of them looking out at the horses.

"*Yah*, he's over there," Hannah said with a knowing look.

"It isn't like that," Patience said.

"No?" Hannah's eyebrows went up, but she didn't look convinced.

"I should go say hello," Patience said.

"*Yah*... But don't be locking yourself to one man in the public eye just yet, my dear," Hannah said meaningfully. "You're young and attractive. We have a few single men who will want to meet you."

Patience forced a smile. "I'm more concerned about how Rue is doing after seeing her Englisher grandmother."

"Ah." Hannah sobered. "That's understandable."

Patience nodded to a few different families as she made her way across the farmyard and toward the horses. Thomas seemed to be deep in thought; neither he nor Rue heard her approach until she was right behind them, and then Thomas startled and turned.

"Hi," she said with a hesitant smile.

"Hi." Thomas relaxed at the sight of her. "How are you?"

Rue grinned up at Patience. "Patience, there's horses. But you can't hug them. That's very dangerous."

Patience chuckled. "It is very dangerous. I see you've been listening to your *daet*."

"I want a horse," Rue said seriously.

"You have horses. Your *daet* has horses that pull the buggy," Patience replied.

"No, I want a horse of my own," she said.

Patience looked over at Thomas and he gave a tired shrug. "Another battle for another day."

"Is everything okay?" Patience asked. "With your *mamm*, I mean. Samuel saw her waiting on a cab, so we know she left, but..."

Thomas licked his lips. "She...says she wants to return to the community."

Patience started to smile. "That's good news!" But when he didn't match her smile, she let it fall. "Isn't it?"

"Rue, do you see those girls at the pump?" Thomas said, pointing. "Why don't you go get some water to drink? I'm sure they'd help you."

Rue ambled off in the direction her father had indicated, and Thomas stood there, his eyes glued to the back of his daughter. She got to the pump and the older girls looked down at her in stunned curiosity—they'd likely just realized this little girl was speaking English, not German. There would be many, many introductions just like that one for little Rue. She'd get used to the initial shock she caused.

"What happened?" Patience asked. "And I won't tell anyone what you tell me, if that's what you're thinking."

"No, I trust you," he said, his gaze flickering down toward her. "The problem is, I don't know what's a good outcome anymore. Two weeks ago, I would have been thanking Gott for my mother's return, and now? I'm worried. She'll be a major influence in my daughter's life— an Englisher *mammi*. Am I raising my daughter just to have her jump the fence the minute she's old enough? Will she stay? If she has a grandmother who did the same..."

"But who came back," she countered.

"But she's still English, and only now do we realize how English she really is..." Thomas stepped a little closer, lowering his voice further. "She's coming back because she misses us, and because she has a granddaughter now."

"Not only for Rue, though," Patience said hopefully.

"No, but Rue factors in rather heavily," Thomas replied seriously. "She wants to help."

They exchanged a meaningful look. She understood his worries very well.

"Oh…" Patience leaned back against the sun-warmed fence, and Thomas did the same, leaving a proper six inches between them. He looked over at her, his dark gaze filled with misery.

"My *mamm* missed the English life so much," he said.

Patience frowned. "People come back when they see the error in their way, and she came back. So she must have seen that the English life was empty and…" Her voice trailed off.

"I don't think it was empty, actually. She's coming back because she realized life is short, and you don't always have the time to repent that you think you do." Thomas sighed. "When she left the first time, it was because she didn't like the restrictions in an Amish life. She said she didn't think Gott requires that, that it only cuts us off from the rest of the believers."

Patience didn't know how to answer that. She rolled the words around in her mind. "But she came back…"

"And if my daughter says something to her about the Amish way not being Gott's will—one day when she's old enough to think she knows it all—what will my *mamm* say to her?" Thomas eyed her for a moment, then shrugged. "I know she's repented and she wants to come back to the narrow path, but will my mother harbor some of those dangerous views still? I might not have cared before I had Rue in my life, but now—"

"Will you turn her away?" Patience asked softly.

"Oh, Patience…" he sighed. "She's my *mamm*! I love her too much to turn her away. But we'll be the ones to pay for it."

"Gott is still working," she said.

"*Yah*…"

"You have to trust that."

"But the right thing to do is often the hard thing, isn't it?" he said.

Was he thinking that the right thing would be to turn away his *mamm*? He didn't elaborate. Right now, the easy thing would be to reach out and take his hand. It would be to lean into his strong shoulder, to comfort him… The easy thing was not the right thing to do.

"But you're good for Rue," he added. "She's doing as well as she is because of you. You're…really good for her."

"I'm not good for you, though," she said.

Thomas dropped his gaze, then shrugged. "You're comforting for me."

Tears misted Patience's eyes. She longed to be his comfort right now, but she knew where that would go. It wasn't only him who was feeling this strong attraction; she was, too, and last night she'd lain awake thinking not of his *mamm* and the drama that had unfolded before him, but of his kiss. His arms around her had felt so warm and safe, and she'd never been kissed quite like that before. She'd never had the experience of feeling heady and grounded all at the same time…

Over at the pump, Amos and Noah stopped for some water, then took Rue's hand. People were moving toward the tent now. It would be time for service to start soon.

"Where will Rue sit?" Patience asked.

Thomas looked toward the tent, then shrugged.

"With me," Thomas replied. "Mary can't chase her down, and she's *mine*. She'll sit with me."

There was no *mamm* to take her to the women's side of the tent, so one little girl would sit on her *daet*'s knee on the men's side—a fair-haired little ray of sunshine amid a sea of males clad in black Sunday clothes. Patience felt a well of compassion for this man and his little girl. They were doing their best together, and she couldn't overstep. She must be available for other men, just in case there was a widower who wanted a wife but no more *kinner*. And Thomas must be available to find a good Amish *mamm* for his daughter.

It was time for service.

Thomas wasn't sure what he expected from his daughter during her very first Amish service. From what he'd gathered already, Rue had never gone to church in her life. Tina had told her a little bit about Gott, a confusing tangle of information that included Heaven for those who had died, but that was the extent of Rue's spiritual education thus far.

Every night, Thomas had been telling her Bible stories, tricking her into listening with rapt attention by beginning each one with "Once upon a time…" It worked. And whenever she asked for another story, he never said no, because she was finally getting the foundation that she so desperately needed.

There was a Bible verse that guided much of Amish parenting: *Train up a child in the way he should go: and when he is old, he will not depart from it.* At least he could give her a reason for her faith—the stories from scripture that could be a bedrock for every choice she made in the future. And if his prayers were answered, those stories would keep her rooted in their faith—*here*.

The raising of a child was such a deep commitment, and he was only now appreciating how much lay on his shoulders as Rue's *daet*.

Thomas sat next to his brother and Amos on the very edge of the bench. If he had to get away from the service for whatever reason, he'd need an exit that didn't cause disruption. Other *daets* sat with their young sons next to them, and he caught their eyes on him. Word would have traveled by now, and he'd already fielded a few questions when they first arrived, but people seemed to know enough from the spread of gossip that they weren't coming forward with more curiosity.

Across the tent, the women's side of the service faced the men's. A couple of single women were looking at him with undisguised interest. He was in need of a wife, and that little detail would have made it into many a kitchen in their community before anyone ever spotted him at service. But he couldn't summon up any interest in other women. The only one he was looking for as he scanned the familiar faces was Patience, and he finally spotted her sitting next to Hannah Kauffman near the front.

Patience caught him looking at her and smiled slightly. What was it about her that made him feel better just by a tiny smile like that one?

"Daddy," Rue said, her voice rising loudly above the murmuring of settling people.

"Shh." Thomas winced and bent his lips down to her ears. "You have to whisper and be very quiet. And please… Call me *daet*."

"That boy has a feather," Rue whispered loudly.

"Rue." He tapped her leg. "Shh."

Rue settled in quietly, but the boy in question turned around, looking at her in open curiosity. His own *daet* tapped his shoulder and he turned back. The feather was confiscated.

The singing started, and Rue was amply drowned out by several hymns, but by the time an elder stood up to pray, Rue was drumming her feet against Thomas's shins and wriggling to get a more comfortable position. She wasn't used to this, and he couldn't blame her, but compared with all the other *kinner* sitting quietly next to their parents on either side of the service, her unruliness stood out.

Would it be appropriate to bring her over to Patience? Would Patience be any better at calming this child than he was? But Rue wasn't Patience's obligation. She was just the teacher next door… And *he* was Rue's *daet*. She was his to raise and guide, and to figure out.

Noah tapped Rue's leg and then passed her a hard candy. Noah had thought of pocketing a few candies? Even Thomas hadn't thought of that. He shot his brother a grateful smile as Rue noisily unwrapped the candy and popped it into her mouth.

By the time the first preacher stood up to speak in German, Thomas knew he was beat. She couldn't understand anything that was being said, and even if she could, it would all be far too complicated for a four-year-old to grasp.

He caught Patience's gaze on him, and he shook his head slightly, letting her know all was well. He couldn't keep leaning on her—it wasn't fair to either of them.

"Come, Rue," he whispered, and he eased off the bench and carried her out of the tent. When he looked back, Noah and Amos were watching him, but they both looked as helpless as he felt.

He was a single *daet* to an Englisher... How was he going to do this?

A few women had some small children playing on a blanket outside the tent.

"Would she like to come play here?" one of the women asked in German.

But Rue didn't speak German, and she didn't obey terribly swiftly, either. Suddenly, leaving her to play with other Amish children felt like it was setting her up for failure. The women would talk about her afterward— the little girl who spoke only English and didn't obey. He didn't want that. Things had already gone wrong with the Smoker family.

"Thank you, but we'll be fine," he said.

Another time, when Rue was more settled maybe. When she'd picked up some German and saw what kind of behavior was expected of the *kinner* here. He'd wait until the people wouldn't judge her harshly, because while there would be kind people who wouldn't, there would be others with less patience of an Englisher child, and he wasn't sure which would be which just yet.

Thomas had been looking forward to seeing Patience today, to spending a little time with her... But maybe it was better to go early. People would start jumping to conclusions, and it would only complicate things. Besides, he wasn't going to be able to hide his feelings for her—he was too tired to manage it. Patience deserved a chance to settle into the Redemption community, free from the taint of the Wiebe men.

"Where are we going, Daddy?" Rue asked as he carried her toward the buggies.

"We're going home," he said.

"How come?"

"Because—" He looked over at her, wondering how to explain the tumble of emotion, his fears, his caution, his exhaustion... "Because I want to."

"Okay." It seemed to be a good enough answer for her, but it wasn't a good answer. Amish looked to their communities to help them through difficult times, and he was pulling back, much like his *mamm* had done when her husband passed away and she'd needed support the most. Was he more like his *mamm* than he liked to admit, too?

The problem was, he didn't want the community's support—he was longing for one woman, and he knew better than to allow his ever-so-observant neighbors to witness that.

Gott, make me a better father. I feel like I'm failing already.

Chapter Eleven

Patience saw Thomas leave the service, and she followed him with her gaze until he disappeared outside the tent. She shouldn't feel so drawn after Thomas and Rue—they weren't hers to worry over—but she couldn't help it. Did he need help with Rue? Should she go out and see?

But there were several women on the bench between her and freedom, and she'd only draw more attention if she had to get past them. So she tried to focus on the service and waited to see if Thomas would come back.

He never did. One sermon turned into singing, and then there was a second sermon. And she did her best to listen to the preachers expound upon scripture, but her heart wasn't in it… It was following after Thomas and his little girl.

Gott, this isn't a good sign if I can't even worship because I'm thinking about him. He isn't for me! I know that. Help me to stop feeling this…

With that kiss, things had changed between them.

For her, she felt even more drawn to the man, and his mother's arrival had made that attraction more dangerous. Thomas was a man without the same deep roots that she had—his *mamm* had jumped the fence, and now Rachel was back in time to help with an Englisher child. Nothing here was easy or straightforward, and maybe that was Gott's way of showing her that Thomas wasn't for her. She might know it logically, but sometimes Gott had to "*bapp* her over the head with it," as her *mamm* would say. So Patience had to admit that Thomas was right in keeping his distance.

Sitting on the bench, her back straight and her thoughts refusing to settle, Patience felt tears welling up inside her. Sunday service wasn't supposed to be about Thomas Wiebe, and she wouldn't let it become that, either. She fixed her mind onto the preacher's words, and tried to find the peace that normally came with worship.

The next day, Patience had Samuel Kauffman give her a ride to the schoolhouse. She hadn't heard from Thomas after service, and all she could assume was that he had things under control. He was Rue's father, after all. He was the one raising the little girl, and it wasn't like there weren't three men in that house to pick up the slack when Mary wasn't able to keep up. Among Thomas, Noah and Amos, they'd figure things out, she was sure.

That was what she told herself, at least. His absence stung, even if she didn't have a right to feel the rejection. They'd talked this over—more than friendship wasn't going to work, so she had no right to expect him to come by just to see her.

The schoolhouse was located on the corner of two rural roads. A field of young wheat rippled across the road from the school, and it was flanked by farmers' fields on either side. Outside, there was some play equipment and some hitching posts in the parking lot. The schoolhouse itself was a squat, white building with a small bell tower on top.

Patience let herself inside with the key she'd been given when she first arrived, and Samuel helped her to unload the school supplies that the community had provided for her.

"Would you like me to stay and help at all?" Samuel asked. "It looks like a lot of work."

"Oh, you're too kind, Samuel," Patience said. "But I'll be fine. Thank you for the offer. I'd rather just putter about on my own and figure out how I want my classroom. It might take me some time to figure out."

Samuel gave her a nod. "No problem. If you need anything, just ring the bell. We can hear it from our place."

The schoolhouse was walking distance—a long walk, mind, but it was doable. When Samuel left, Patience set to work with some cloths and cleaning supplies, scrubbing the room from top to bottom.

Back in Beaufort, she and her *mamm* had shopped for some classroom decorations—paper birthday balloons for each student's birthday, some hangable signs with multiplication tables, some math equations, some sight words for new readers that they had picked up at the dollar store… She would be teaching everything from the first grade through to the eighth, and while she had books to show her what information needed to be covered for each grade, it was daunting, to say the least.

Patience wiped down the last windowsill, cleansing away dust and a few dead flies, leaving the entire room smelling of Pine-Sol and possibilities. Just as she wiped off the last windowsill, there was a knock at the front door, and she startled. She wasn't expecting anyone.

Patience went to the door and pulled it open, and she couldn't help but smile when she saw Thomas standing there with Rue at his side. Rue had her hands folded in front of her and an excited smile on her face.

"Hello, Rue!" Patience said, then she looked up at Thomas. "Hi, Thomas…"

A smile tickled the corners of his lips. "We wanted to see if you needed help."

So he'd come to see her after all, and she felt a sudden rush of relief that whatever they'd shared wasn't completely changed and forgotten. But then another possibility occurred to her—this was Monday, after all. Was he here for a favor?

"Do you need me to watch her while you work?" she asked.

"No, I took the day off," Thomas replied. "With Rue settling in still, Amos and Noah said they could handle things on their own for today."

"I would have offered to watch her," Patience said. "I did agree to help you out. It's just… I thought you… were finished with me."

"Finished—" Thomas swallowed. "No, not at all. I just—"

They stared at each other, without the words to capture it all, then Rue broke the moment by brushing past Patience and heading toward one of the boxes of supplies that sat on a desk. She stood up onto her tiptoes to look inside.

"Rue, do you want to play with some of that modeling dough?" Patience asked. "You can take it to one of the desks, if you want to."

Rue liked this idea, and she grabbed a pot of red dough and went to a desk on the far side of the room next to the teacher's desk.

"Daddy, I'm in school!" Rue announced.

Thomas smiled in his daughter's direction, then turned his gaze back to Patience. "I didn't mean to seem like I was pushing you off. It's just been complicated lately, and I'm trying not to take advantage of our friendship here. I'm sure there are other men you'd like to meet."

"Not really," she admitted.

"Fine, then other friends you'd like to make. I'm sorry, I didn't mean to come off as…a jerk."

Patience shrugged. "Of course not."

Obviously, they both had been afraid of overstepping, and knowing that helped.

"So, you wanted to help?" she asked.

"*Yah.* That was the plan."

Patience pulled out a box of supplies. "I need to get these organized in the bins up there at the front. I'm thinking I can have all the markers, glue and scissors in those bins, and when the *kinner* need them, I can pass them out."

"Sure." Thomas easily lifted the heavy box.

"I could have helped you during the service, you know," Patience said as they headed toward the front of the classroom.

"I felt like I should do it myself," Thomas said. "After I kissed you, I mean. I know I ruined things there, and I didn't want you to think I was taking advantage or..."

"I don't think that," she said.

"Are we becoming more to each other?" Thomas asked, turning toward her. He put the box down on a desktop.

"Maybe we are," she admitted.

"The thing is," he said quietly, "I'm the one at fault here. I'm feeling things I shouldn't. You're beautiful, and I'm attracted to you. I'm just trying to pretend that I'm not. I think it's the smart thing to do. It just gets a bit awkward sometimes."

Patience felt warmth hit her cheeks. He'd called her beautiful again... No other man had told her that before. Even Ruben had called her "good-looking" and "strong." Not beautiful. Beautiful was different... It came from a different place.

"I'll never have my own *kinner*, Thomas," she reminded him. "I'd be happy to help out with Rue. She needs someone who can love her for who she is, and one of these days soon, if I stay in Redemption as a teacher, I'll have her in my classroom. So, don't be afraid of taking advantage. Really, you're just giving me a chance to be more than a teacher to one little girl. I won't have that offer very often."

"Yah?" His gaze softened. "You sure about that?"

"Positive. I can be your friend, Thomas. I'm going to be the old maid schoolteacher, so I'll need friends."

"Don't say that," he chuckled.

"I've very nearly made my peace with it," she said with a shrug. "I'll get there."

"There might be a widower—" he started, but Patience shook her head, and he fell silent.

"I tried that once," she said. "It didn't work for me, and I'm not in a rush to embarrass myself or a good man in that way again."

"Just tell me if I'm overstepping, or asking for too much when it comes to Rue," he said. "Because I don't want to ruin the friendship we have. You mean a lot to me."

"Okay."

She'd try to keep her feelings in line with her rational expectations. She'd stop hoping to hear from him when he didn't need her help with something. She could be reasonable when she needed to be.

Patience filled the first bin with markers, and the second with rulers and protractors for the higher grades' math. And when she turned for the box again, she nearly collided with Thomas. He was pulling out a bundle of rulers, and they both froze.

Thomas was so close that she could feel the fabric of his shirt touch her dress—that soft scrape of cotton against cotton. She sucked in a breath, and he smelled musky with a hint of shaved wood. That smell had

seeped into her over the last while—a scent she asso-
ciated with this carpenter *daet*—and it made her heart
ache.

She felt his work-roughened hand brush against hers,
and he moved one finger up her skin in a slow line. Her
breath caught, every fiber of her being focused on that
one place on her body. She knew she should move back,
move her hand at the very least… But she couldn't quite
bring herself to do it. She lifted her fingers toward him,
and he twined his through hers. They didn't move—
not toward each other, and not away, just standing there
breathing the same air, their hands clasped.

What was it about this man that made her do this?
Why did something as simple as standing this close to
him, or touching his hand, feel like it could stop the
entire earth from spinning?

But then Thomas did what she wasn't strong enough
to do on her own, and he let go of her hand and took a
deliberate step back. She released a shaky sigh.

"We have to be more careful," she whispered.

"Yah…" He cleared his throat.

She missed him—even standing right here next to
him, she missed his fingers twined through hers—and
all she could think about was the feeling of his lips, his
arms around her, the tickle of his stubble against her
face… But she had to stop this. Whatever they were
feeling had no future. Why was she punishing herself
like this?

"Why don't I get those chairs from the corner? That's
across the room."

She smiled at his dry humor. "Maybe a better idea."

He caught her gaze with an impish grin.

"I made a family," Rue announced from her seat at the desk. There were four blobs of modeling dough lined up. "They're Amish. You can tell because they have a rooster named Toby."

"Yah?" Thomas said. "And who else is there?"

"That's a *mammi*," Rue said. "And that's a *daet*."

Patience looked over at Thomas, her heart suspended in her throat. Rue had used the Amish words for a grandmother and father... And it was her representation of a family. She saw that Thomas's eyes misted.

"And who is the other one?" he asked, his voice catching.

"That's just me. I'm next to Toby."

"Yah, I can see that," he said. "Right next to Toby."

"He's part of the family, Daddy," Rue said seriously. "I just want you to remember that we don't eat family."

Thomas burst out laughing. "No, we don't." He turned to Patience with a rueful smile. "I'm stuck with that rooster until it dies of old age, you know."

And he was, Patience had to agree, all because a little girl loved a scruffy, bad-tempered rooster. It was amazing what the love of a little girl could do.

That evening, after Rue was already asleep in her little bed with the curtains pulled shut to block out the last of the summer sunlight, Thomas sat on the steps of the house, a piece of wood in his hands, and he whittled away at it. Rue had given him an idea, and he was now working on some little wooden Amish people—a *mammi*, a *daet* and even two uncles. But right now, he was working on the *mammi*. Wood curled as his knife pared away another slice of wood, and he blew on it, scattering the shavings into the summer wind.

The funny thing was, as he worked on what was supposed to be the *mammi*, the figure was turning more slender, more lithe and much more like a *mamm* in a family... He didn't carve a face, but the figure was one he recognized—this looked very much like Patience. Would anyone else notice that? What was it about this woman that had crept into his head, coming out in his work?

Because he couldn't stop thinking about her... And that was wrong, because he had to put his daughter first. She hadn't asked to be born, and yet here she was, thrust into a world that must seem incredibly foreign to her. She was trying to adjust—he could see that—but the burden couldn't rest on those tiny shoulders. He was her *daet*, and he had to smooth the way for her.

A buggy turned into the drive, and he looked up in the lowering light. He recognized Bishop Glick with the reins in his hands, and he was alone. The sun was near setting, and the shadows were long and soft. Thomas put down his carving, then rose to his feet and headed toward the bishop's buggy.

"Good evening, Bishop!" Thomas said, as he ambled over. "How are you doing tonight?"

"Well, I'm enjoying this dry weather," the bishop replied. "After all that rain last month, it feels good to have dry feet."

"*Yah*, it does," Thomas said with a nod. "What can I do for you?"

"Well… This affects both you and your brother, so maybe I should discuss it with the both of you."

"Mamm?" he asked.

"Yah." The bishop tied off his reins and hopped down from his buggy. "Your *mamm* came to speak with me, and… I thought it best to come see you about it."

Thomas led the way inside, and Amos and Mammi both greeted the bishop with smiles, but when his intention to talk with Thomas and Noah was made clear, they excused themselves and left the three in privacy.

The sitting room was lit by a kerosene lamp hanging on a hook overhead. There was another reading lamp between the couch and a chair, and the bishop took the chair, his expression solemn.

"Our *mamm* came to talk to us," Noah admitted.

"Yah, I understand that," the bishop agreed. "And she did come see me. She wants to return."

"A little late," Noah muttered.

"Are you angry still, then?" Bishop Glick asked.

"You could say that," Noah admitted.

"And now that she's wanting to come back," the bishop said, "will you give her a home when she returns?"

"Yah," Thomas interjected. "I will, at least. Of course."

"Can you forgive her, though?" the older man asked. "Both of you. Can you offer her your sincere forgiveness for her past mistakes?"

Thomas looked over at his brother and they exchanged a silent, miserable stare. Forgiveness wasn't quite so easy to deliver.

"We'll try," Thomas replied after a beat of silence.

"You left the service early on Sunday," the bishop said. "I wanted to ask you why. The sermon was about forgiving others, and—"

"It wasn't because of the sermon topic," Thomas replied. "Rue isn't used to worship, yet. Bishop, I'm doing my best. She hasn't been raised in our community from babyhood. There is a lot for her to learn—for both of us. We'll need a little grace."

"Your *mamm* said something quite similar," the bishop said, his voice low. "She said she's made mistakes, and all she could hope for at this point was a little grace and forgiveness."

Tears misted in Thomas's eyes and he swallowed, blinking hard. His *mamm*… Facing life as a single parent was not easy, but she'd left them! She'd given them an impossible choice, and she'd gone alone to the city, to her sister and to that life that they'd been taught was fraught with evil.

"This is the part that is difficult for me," the bishop went on. "If we vote to let her come back, then we're opening our community to her influence. We all influence each other, whether we like it or not. But if I turn her away, then perhaps I'm going against Gott's will. He asks us to forgive, not to judge, and Gott works in mysterious ways. He's brought his wayward daughter to our door. She's asked to be permitted to live a plain life again. What do we do with that?"

Thomas licked his lips, but he remained silent.

"What would you like us to do under these circumstances?" the bishop pressed. "This is your *mamm*. You must have missed her desperately."

"*Yah*, we've missed her," Noah confirmed.

"As her *kinner*, your lives will be directly affected by this decision," the bishop said. "This will be voted on by the elders, but I'd like you both to give us an idea of how it would impact you if she returned, or if she stayed away. To have your *mamm* back in your life would be wonderful, I'm sure. But it would also impact your daughter, Thomas. I wanted to hear from you what you would like the outcome to be."

"You want us to be part of the decision?" Noah asked.

"Indirectly, yes. I want you to let us know how you feel about your *mamm*'s return. And then we will pray for Gott's guidance, and vote. But your feelings in this matter to us."

"I don't know what to say just now," Thomas admitted. He loved his *mamm*, but he also loved his daughter. There was a grave risk in his *mamm*'s return, and yet... It was another impossible choice. How could a man be asked to choose between his child and his *mamm*?

"You'll need to talk as brothers," the older man said. "So you can tell me in a few days, then."

The bishop took his leave, shaking both of their hands before he went back out to his waiting buggy. Thomas and Noah went back onto the porch and Thomas picked up his whittling again. Together he and his brother stared out at the dusky sky. Bugs circled the kerosene lamp that gave Thomas enough light by which to work, and for a few minutes they were both silent.

"I am angry," Noah said quietly. "And I'm insulted that she doesn't believe what she taught us anymore. But all the same, I want her back. Maybe even to argue with her about all we went through—maybe just for that."

Thomas sucked in a wavery breath. His experience of their *mamm*'s life with the Englishers was different, because he'd joined her there for a few years. He knew what she'd experienced out there—it was a whole different way of seeing things, and when you were out there in the midst of the Englishers, their ways didn't seem so wrong. It was a strange experience.

"I miss Mamm," Thomas said quietly. "But will she make an Englisher life look that much more appealing to my daughter?"

"If Mamm stays English, it might give Rue somewhere to go to," Noah replied.

"I hadn't thought of that…" Thomas worked at the details of the *kapp* and hair on his little figurine, the work calming the clamor in his head. There was no clear path here—no easy decision that protected his daughter's innocence. His own mistakes were shadowing him here, as were his *mamm*'s.

"Is this cruel of the bishop to ask our input?" Noah asked.

"Maybe," Thomas said. "But we're the ones who will live with the impact of her return most closely. Maybe it's just wise of them to listen to what we have to say."

"So what *do* we say?" Noah looked up at his brother.

Thomas turned back to his whittling, his heart heavy. He didn't want to sit here—he wanted to get away from the house and get alone with his thoughts. He needed to walk.

"Maybe we just say that we love our *mamm*," Thomas said. "It's the only thing we can be sure is true."

Noah swatted at a mosquito on his arm, and Thomas tucked his whittling aside, snapped his knife shut and put it back into his pocket.

"I need to clear my head," Thomas said. "I'm going to take a walk."

"*Yah*, okay," Noah replied, and he sucked in a deep breath.

And Thomas headed off across the lawn and toward the gravel drive. The sun was bleeding red along the horizon, and his heart was bleeding within him.

Gott, I can't choose between my daughter and my mamm. And I can't read the future, either. What do I do? What do I say? Can You redeem this mess that we've made?

Chapter Twelve

Patience sat on the edge of her bed up in the guest room of the Kauffmans' home. The older folks were downstairs in the sitting room. She could hear the murmur of their voices through the floorboards, but her attention wasn't on their muffled conversation. She was looking outside the window at the slowly setting sun. It flooded the sky with crimson, matching her mood tonight.

She'd thought that talking things through with Thomas would be enough to banish whatever they were feeling for each other, but it hadn't worked—not in the schoolhouse, at least. Her hand tingled where he'd touched it, and she balled her fingers into a fist.

She had to stop this! Whatever was sparking between them couldn't last. She didn't think he meant to toy with her, any more than she meant to toy with him. But she was no longer a young thing with giddy hopes of romance. She didn't have what a man like Thomas needed, and adults with responsibilities were obligated to be practical.

She couldn't relax, and while she'd get used to living with the Kauffmans this year, it wasn't like being at home with her *mamm* and *daet*. If she were home right now, they'd all be sitting around the kitchen table talking about the latest gossip in the community, or playing a game of Dutch Blitz. Being with family was easier, even if she was the last one left at home.

She'd wanted this move to a new community—desperately. And now that she was here, she felt nothing but homesick.

Patience sucked in a breath. Maybe a walk would do her good, clear her head, give her some fresh air and a bit of perspective again.

She headed down the stairs, and when she got to the bottom of the staircase, she poked her head into the sitting room.

"Oh, hello, dear," Hannah said with a smile. "Are you hungry?"

"No," Patience said and smiled in return. Hannah seemed to feed people on instinct—whenever she saw them, she offered a snack. "But thank you. I thought I'd go for a walk."

"Oh, of course. Enjoy yourself."

Samuel smiled, too, then passed the folded newspaper over to his wife. "Look who's gotten married—that's old Ben's grandson, isn't it? Ben Yoder—the one who built that silo, and the storm crushed it, remember? His son, with the one leg a bit shorter than the other..."

Patience went back through the kitchen and out the side door, the sound of the older couple's discussion whether this was the right young man in question or someone with a similar name following her until she got out onto the step. This old couple knew the family stories of everyone, it seemed. That's how a close community worked, and it was that very intimate community knowledge that she'd been trying to escape in Beaufort.

She sucked in a deep breath, the aroma of lilacs and freshly cut grass soothing her nerves, and she angled her steps across the lawn and toward the field. She wanted to walk and pray and feel like there might be a purpose in her life again. Because after Ruben, whom she hadn't really loved, but whom she respected a great deal…and now after Thomas, whom she'd started to feel things for that she had no right to feel, she just wanted the solace that only Gott could give her.

But Gott wasn't soothing her heart! He wasn't taking these feelings away! Why not? She was trying to do the right thing—not to toy with something so powerful as this kind of attraction between a man and a woman—and Gott wasn't doing what everyone assured her He would do if she just took a step in the right direction. Gott was not making this easier.

The grass was long and lush. There was only about two acres between the Kauffman house and the fence at the end of their property, but Patience liked this walk—wildflowers mingling with grass, the birds twittering their good-nights in the copses of trees, and the warm wind reminding her that there was still life on the other side of loss.

As she came within sight of the wooden fence that separated the two properties, she saw a figure standing there, head down, shoulders stooped, leaning against the top rail. It was Thomas—she'd know him anywhere. She slowed her stride, wondering if she should turn back. He lifted his head, looking out toward the sunset— away from her and to her left. What was he doing out here—the same as her? No one walked out this direction unless they wanted privacy, and it wouldn't be right to interrupt his, and yet—

Thomas turned then as if on instinct—and he seemed to have spotted her, because he straightened.

"Patience?" he said, his voice surfing the breeze toward her.

She couldn't turn back now, and if she had to be utterly truthful, she didn't want to.

"I just came for a walk," she said, closing the distance between them. They stood on either side of the wooden fence, the grass rippling around her as she looked into Thomas's pain-filled face.

"Are you okay?" she asked.

"I'm…just thinking, I guess," he said. "Are you?"

Did her own misery show on her face, too? "I'm praying," she said.

"What are you praying for?" he asked.

"Comfort," she said. She didn't want to tell him that she was praying for Gott to empty her heart of whatever it was she was feeling for him.

Thomas leaned against the fence. It came up only to just below his chest, and he reached for her hand. She came closer and reached out, and he caught her fingers in his strong grip. It was a relief to have this contact with him, and she shut her eyes for a moment, wishing she didn't feel it.

"I missed you," Thomas said, his voice low and gruff.

"Thomas..."

"I know, I know," he said. "I'm supposed to turn this off, aren't I? I'm supposed to recognize that it won't work and do the honorable thing."

"Yes!" she said. "We both are! What are we, if we aren't honorable?"

Patience took a step closer. The fence loomed between them, the grass tickling her legs, and she looked down at his work-worn fingers moving over hers.

"Have you managed to stop feeling this?" he asked.

"No," she whispered. "But I'm praying for it... Oh, how I'm praying..."

Tears misted her eyes and she swallowed hard. Thomas released her fingers and she pulled her hand against her apron. She didn't know what to say. She had no words of wisdom here, no answers that would fix this problem for them.

"You're all I seem to think about," Thomas said. "And when I see you, I—I don't know even know how to explain it. It's like I can't be content until I've held your hand, or...kissed you."

"But Thomas, you know what you need... And I've already turned down one man because I can't live my life being the second best he settled for. I can't be that for you, either."

"Should we avoid each other, then?" he murmured.

"Maybe..." But the very thought was a painful one. It would hurt for a long time, but eventually, she'd find her balance again.

"The bishop came to visit tonight," Thomas said.

"The bishop? Why?" she breathed. Had gossip already spread? Had someone seen them together? Possibilities tumbled through her head, and she couldn't help but feel that welling sense of guilt. A couple couldn't play with these things. Especially not the schoolteacher!

"It was about my *mamm*," he said.

"Oh…"

He gave her a brief overview of the bishop's visit and his request for their input, and then he heaved a sigh. "I can't ask the bishop to turn my *mamm* away, and yet, I'm scared for Rue."

"You'll raise Rue right," Patience said, but even as the words came out of her mouth, she knew it wasn't enough.

"I'll need to get married," he said, and his voice caught.

Patience stared up at him. She could hear in his voice that it wasn't her that he'd wed, either. He'd have to find someone who could give him *kinner* to fill in those gaps in his home.

"*Yah*, you will," she said, trying to sound braver than she felt. "It will be okay."

"Will it?" he asked. "Really?"

"I think you need to—" she started.

"No, tell me how you *feel* about it," he interrupted her. "Because I've been thinking myself in circles. What really matters here is how we feel."

"No!" she snapped. "No! I'm not doing that, because it isn't fair! I hate it, okay? I hate it! And I won't go to your wedding, either!"

"Good. At least you hate it as much as I do."

Thomas reached for her hand again and pulled her up against the fence. He dipped his head down and caught her lips with his. His kiss was sad, and filled with longing. She let her eyes flutter shut, leaning against that rough wood that held them apart as he kissed her tenderly. When he pulled back, she opened her eyes again and found him looking down at her miserably.

The sun had set now, the last smudge of red along the horizon, and they stood there in the growing darkness, a fence between them, and her heart aching in her chest.

"How am I supposed to just walk away from the woman I love?" he whispered.

The breath whisked out of her lungs as the words hit her.

"You love me?" she whispered.

Thomas looked at the fence between them irritably. "*Yah*, I do."

Thomas climbed the fence, and then vaulted himself over the other side. He tugged her into his arms and pulled her close. She could feel his face against her hair, the stubble on his cheek scraping against the stiff cotton of her *kapp*. It felt good to have his arms around her, his heart beating strong against her.

"The question is," he said, his voice low and gravelly, "do you love me?"

Patience felt the tears rise up inside her. She'd been fighting this for longer than she'd realized. This man had managed to slip beneath her cautious defenses, and she'd fallen for him. She'd been praying and praying for Gott to take this away, but… It was too late.

"Yah," she whispered. "I do."

The inevitable heartbreak she was trying to protect herself from had arrived. She'd fallen in love with him in spite of all her best efforts. And now all she could do was pray that Gott would take her through.

The dusky darkness was growing ever deeper, and Thomas looked around them. In the distance, the Kauffman house's downstairs windows glowed with light from the gas lamps, but it felt far away, and the chill of oncoming autumn whispered through the grass. He'd been standing out here praying for some sort of insight, some wisdom that could come only from Gott, and instead he'd come face-to-face with the woman he couldn't seem to get out of his system.

Was she his answer? Dare he hope it? Thomas cupped her cheek with one hand, and she leaned into his touch. Her skin was so soft, and her eyes glittered in the lowering light. She loved him... Somehow, he hadn't expected her to admit it. But he wasn't alone in this ocean of emotion—she loved him, too! His heart welled up inside his chest. If she loved him, there was hope, wasn't there? He wasn't just some foolish man pining for a woman who didn't see him the same way. This was different...

"You love me," he repeated. "Then let's find a way."

"What way?" she asked.

"So I'm supposed to find someone else?" he whispered.

"Yah." Her voice sounded strangled.

"And if I want you?"

"I want you, too… But it isn't about that, is it? Do you think I want to be the one who holds you back from the full life of a growing family?" Patience demanded, her voice strengthening. "You seem to think this is about your sacrifice only, but I'm not the kind of woman who can give a man *half* the life he wants and figure I've done well for myself. Getting a husband is a fine accomplishment, but marriage is about a whole lot more than a wedding, because after the excitement and when things calm down again, you'd still want *kinner.* You'll still *need* them! That isn't going away. And when women in our community got pregnant, women I've made quilts with, I'd constantly wonder what you were thinking, because I would know that you settled for me. I wouldn't be sure if I was enough, after all."

Enough! Could she even wonder that?

"You would be," he insisted.

"No!" She took a step back. "No, Thomas! I have older sisters. I've seen the rhythm of marriage. It starts out passionately where nothing else matters but the two of them, but a family matters. And your needs won't go away. Neither will Rue's."

Rue… She was the one he needed to worry about, and Patience had made a painfully accurate point. He was afraid that he wouldn't be able to give his daughter enough reason to stay Amish, to stay with *him*… But there was an Amish proverb that said, *Don't bother telling your child what to do, she'll only copy your actions anyway.*

And what would Rue do as an only child in an Amish community? She'd be different in two ways then—born

English, and having no siblings at home. She needed stability, and it was very difficult to achieve that when Thomas couldn't give her what all the other Amish *kinner* would have. When she got to be a teen, she'd do what her own *daet* had done—she'd launch herself out into the unknown, away from the community, away from her *daet*. He'd lose her, and he couldn't take that chance.

"It won't work," he breathed.

"No, it won't." Patience's chin quivered.

How much heartbreak had this woman gone through already? He hated being the cause of more pain for her, but sometimes love wasn't about a feeling. Sometimes love had to be broader and deeper. It had to persevere and sacrifice, and it had to do the right thing, even when it didn't want to. He had to be a *daet* first. He'd brought Rue into this world, and Gott had brought her home to him. He could no longer follow his own heart when it came to the woman he longed to be with, not when being with her would jeopardize his daughter.

A child was a gift from Gott, and she was lent to him for only a little while. He'd never forgive himself if he let his daughter go in order to satisfy his own romantic longings. Whatever his daughter chose when she grew up, he had to know that he'd done his very best by her and have no regrets to haunt him in his old age.

"I'm still going to love you, even if we can't make this work," he said huskily.

"*Yah*, me, too…" Her voice was thick was tears.

"So what do we do?" he asked.

"We carry on," she said hollowly. "We put one foot in

front of the other, and we put our backs into our work. That's what we do. We can't be the first couple to realize they loved each other but there was no hope. And we won't be the last."

Maybe not, but it felt like the universe began and ended in their feelings for each other, as foolish as that might be.

Thomas looked toward the Kauffmans' house with the lights shining from the windows in the distance. A car swept down the rural road, headlights cutting through the darkness, and then a pickup truck came thundering afterward, Englisher teenagers whooping out the windows.

That was the foolish life he was trying to keep his daughter away from, but more immediately, whooping, half-drunk Englishers were also the kind of danger he needed to protect Patience from this evening. The sky was almost fully dark now, and he couldn't let Patience walk to the Kauffman house alone—for safety's sake.

"Let me get you home," he said, and he caught her hand in his.

She squeezed his hand in return.

"We shouldn't—" she started.

"Let me get you home," he repeated, his voice low. "And then I won't touch you again, or ask you to love me. I'll let you focus on your work. I won't make this harder on you. But just for now… Let me hold your hand."

"Okay," she whispered.

And they walked through that long, lush grass together as the moon started to rise and the first pricks of stars materialized overhead. Her hand was warm and soft in his grasp, and he wished that this walk, and these stars and that crescent of a moon could last forever. Because while his heart was breaking, at least he had her at his side and his goodbye could be postponed.

When they got to the gate, he stopped, and she opened it, hovering for a breathless moment as if she might come back into his arms.

"Good night," she said, her voice broken.

"Good night," he replied.

The front door opened and Samuel appeared, light from indoors spilling out onto the porch. Patience picked up her pace, and Thomas waved at Samuel, trying to act like this was nothing more than a friendly walk—like no hearts had been shattered this evening.

Patience got to the door, and he held his breath.

Look back... Look at me...

But she didn't. She disappeared inside, and the door shut behind them, leaving Thomas alone in the darkness.

He couldn't ask her to continue loving him. If he cared for her at all, he'd pray for Gott to rinse him out of her heart completely. But he couldn't pray for that for himself. He wanted to remember... Because in all his life, he'd never loved a woman like this.

Chapter Thirteen

Patience stood at the window in the laundry room and watched as Thomas disappeared into the darkness. The older folks wouldn't look for her here—not at this time of night—and all she wanted right now was a moment or two to try to collect herself. She'd cry upstairs alone, but she'd have to pass the Kauffmans to get up there. She wrapped her arms around her waist, tears welling up inside her. She loved him… And it wouldn't work. She'd never felt this way before. She'd had a few crushes, and had even accepted a proposal based on profound respect, but what she felt for Thomas was deeper and broader and cut much more sharply at the realization that it could never happen.

She realized now that falling in love with Thomas hadn't been a choice—hadn't even been avoidable. Whatever they felt for each other was something outside their ability to wisely sidestep. How was this fair? Gott asked them to walk the narrow path—to do right when the rest of the world took the easy way. And she was doing her best to do right—to put Rue and Rachel ahead of her own deepest desire. There should be some comfort in knowing she'd done the right thing, and yet all she could feel right now were the cracks in her heart.

"Patience, dear?"

Patience wiped her eyes and turned to see Hannah in the doorway. Hannah held a kerosene lamp, lighting up the laundry room in a cheery glow. Her plump figure was illuminated—an impeccably white apron against a gray dress. She squinted through her glasses.

"I'm sorry, Hannah, I'm just a little emotional," Patience said. She turned away again, blinking back her tears.

"I'm sure that some pie would help," Hannah said.

"Not this time," Patience said, and she wiped at her cheeks again. "I'll be fine."

"Is that the Wiebe boy?" Hannah asked.

"Uh… He walked me home. It got dark faster than I thought, and—" She couldn't lie, so she stopped. There was so much more to the story, but it was private.

"And you've had some sort of lover's spat?" Hannah pressed.

How obvious had their relationship been? They'd done their best to hide it—especially at Sunday service.

"I was helping with Rue," she said.

"And falling in love, I dare say," Hannah replied.

"It's not that—" It was so much more than that. "We're not engaged. There's no agreement between us…"

"Ah, but so much happens before those understandings, doesn't it?" Hannah asked. "A heart gets entangled before any proposals come along. Come now. I know you want to go upstairs and have a cry, but I'm going to suggest something else that works much better. Come to my table and have a cry there. I'll bring you some pie and we'll talk it all out. It might not fix what's gone wrong with your young man, but it will start the healing that much faster, I can tell you that."

Patience paused to consider. Hannah seemed to understand a whole lot more than Patience even realized, and if she were at home with her own *mamm* right now, she'd likely do the same. Except, she and her *mamm* liked to take walks together—walking and talking, and sorting out all the things that seemed so impossible on her own.

Tears spilled down Patience's cheeks, and Hannah reached out, took her hand and led her down the hallway and into the kitchen. Hannah left the lamp on the table, then passed a handkerchief to Patience.

"Let it out, dear," Hannah said softly. "I'm going to whip you some cream to go on top of your pie. I think you could use a little treat…"

Patience felt the tears rise again, and this time she didn't stop them. She lowered her head onto her arms and cried.

Tuesday morning, school was set to open and Samuel waited patiently by the door, the buggy hitched and ready. When Patience brought her last bag of school supplies to the door, Samuel took it from her and put it up on his shoulder.

"All ready, Mamm!" Samuel called. "I'll be back in a short while."

"Drive safe, Daet. And you have a good day with those *kinner*, Patience," Hannah said.

Samuel carried her bag out to the buggy and Patience got settled in her seat while Samuel put the bag in the back and came around to hoist himself up.

"It's a beautiful morning," Samuel said, flicking the reins.

And it was—warm, bright and a cloudless sky. But it was hard to feel cheery this morning. A good cry last night, and another one upstairs in her bed, had drained her of tears, but her heart still felt heavy in her chest.

"How many *kinner* do you have, Samuel?" Patience asked, more by way of making conversation than by any real interest.

"Oh…" Samuel's cheeks pinked. "None, I'm afraid."

Patience looked over at him, surprised. "But you called her Mamm."

"And she called me Daet. I know…" He sighed. "You see, we wanted *kinner*—a whole house filled with them—but Gott never gave us any. We were heartbroken about it for years, and then we remembered that Gott doesn't make mistakes. He brought us together, gave us a love like no other and didn't choose to give us *kinner* to love. So we decided to look at it differently."

A love like no other, and an inability to bring children into the marriage. She could identify with that a little too keenly.

"How?" Patience asked.

"We decided to be the *mamm* and *daet* that young

people needed when their own parents were far from them," Samuel replied. "We've had traveling students stay with us. A few Englisher college students came to see how we Amish live and we gave them room and board. We also opened our home to the teachers." Samuel cast her a shy smile. "In hopes that we could be a little piece of home when you are far from yours."

"That's...beautiful," she said.

A life of meaning, even without *kinner* of their own. She'd been wanting to create something like that for her own life—a loving teacher to help guide these *kinner* toward Gott, even if she never did have any babies of her own.

"Can I ask you something, Samuel?" she asked hesitantly.

"*Yah*, you can ask," Samuel replied.

"Did you ever...lose your faith in Gott's leading? Gott led you to Hannah—and I believe that—but did you ever, in a moment of weakness, regret your marriage? Did you ever think that if you'd married someone else, you might have had that houseful of *kinner* after all?"

Samuel looked over at her, his eyebrows raised, and she felt a flood of shame at even asking him such a thing.

"I know it's a terrible question," she said quickly. "I don't mean to disrespect your marriage, or your wife."

"Not once," he said quietly. "And that is not just the answer of a loyal husband. That is the honest truth. My wife is a wonderful woman, as you probably already know. And being her husband—that was Gott moving. I have never questioned that. And what Gott has joined—"

"—let no man put asunder," she finished for him.

"*Yah*, that, too," he said. "But I was going to say, what Gott has joined, He joins for good reason. No one can love me just like my Hannah. And no one can love her just like me. And I'm grateful every day for the woman Gott gave me. *Yah*, I missed out on being a *daet* to my own little ones, but we remind each other that we're still able to love the ones Gott puts in our paths. When we were younger, we focused on the *kinner*. And as we aged, so did the ones we reached out to. It happened naturally, I suppose. So she calls me Daet and I call her Mamm. Because we still have a job to do—it's just a little harder."

The horses clopped along, early morning dew shining like diamonds on the tall grasses in the ditches on either side of the road. Samuel hummed a little song to himself, and Patience's heart pounded in her chest.

Here was a couple that had never had *kinner*, had never resented each other for the loss, and had made life so meaningful and rich that she'd never have guessed their childless state if he hadn't told her himself.

She'd been so certain that Thomas would regret giving up that houseful of *kinner* of his own... But was it possible that he might not? Could this love that had blossomed between them be something wonderful enough that he'd never regret the day he chose her?

But as soon as the hope started to rise up inside her, she remembered that this wasn't just about Thomas and a desire for children. This was about the daughter he already had—the little girl who needed her roots, her stability and a family that could anchor her to an Amish life.

Even if Patience could take the leap for a love like theirs, she knew what Rue needed, and she still couldn't provide it.

Samuel pulled the buggy to a stop in front of the schoolhouse, and Patience took out the key. She was here, ready to teach her very first day of school—and she'd have to find a way to fill that aching hole in her heart alone.

"Let me get that bag for you," Samuel said.

"Oh, I can get it," she said, forcing a smile.

"Now, now," Samuel said gently. "Let an old man treat you right, my dear. It does me good."

And she realized that it did. By showing kindness to a new teacher who was very near the age his own *kinner* would have been, she was letting him be the *daet* he'd so longed to be. So she let Samuel pull the bag out of the back of the buggy and carry it into the schoolhouse for her. Then he headed back out to his waiting buggy and was on his way again.

Patience stood in the center of the schoolroom, the air cool and quiet, and lifted her heart to Gott.

Give me purpose, she pleaded. *I have so much love to give, and no one to take it. I might not ever have a family of my own, if that is Your will, but give me purpose and people to love, anyway.*

This was her classroom—may Gott bless the *kinner* who passed through these doors, and may Gott fill her aching, lonely heart.

* * *

Thomas left Rue with Mary that day, with some solemn promises on Rue's part to obey the older woman without question.

"All right?" he'd asked her. "You do as Mammi says. If I come home and find out that you haven't…"

"Then what?" Rue whispered.

And he really didn't have an answer to that, so instead he shook his finger meaningfully, bent down to kiss the top of her head and headed out to work.

His mind wasn't on the bedroom set he was building, though. He knew the work well enough that he didn't need to think too much about it as his hands went through the motions. He was sanding and getting the wood ready for the first layer of stain.

Thomas rubbed the sandpaper over the headboard, back and forth, a fragrant powder of wood falling to the ground and clinging to his pants and the hairs on his forearms. He normally felt calmed and soothed in his work, but today his heart seemed to beat with the weight of all his grief.

He loved her… Oh, how he loved her…

But he needed a *mamm* for his daughter and a family of his own, and yet his heart couldn't let go of the woman he'd so recklessly fallen in love with.

The day crawled by, and Amos and Noah took care of customers and let him stay in the back workroom, avoiding people for the rest of the day.

But then in the afternoon, Noah came into the workshop.

"Thomas, Ben Smoker wanted to talk to you," he said.

Ben Smoker—the family that didn't want his daughter to play with their girls. Susan had made herself clear enough to Patience, and Ben had stood behind his wife. Rue was too much of a danger for their *kinner*, it seemed, and the last week had left Thomas with a tender spot in his heart when it came to the way his daughter had been treated.

Thomas stopped the sanding and shook the wood powder off his arms. "What does he want?"

"He just—" Noah started, but then fell silent when Ben appeared at his side.

"Thomas, how are you?" Ben asked with a friendly smile, but when he saw Thomas's face, the smile faltered. Thomas hadn't even bothered to try to look friendly. He didn't have the energy today.

"I'm fine. You?" Thomas asked, forcing the pleasantries out.

"Look," Ben said, coming closer and glancing over his shoulder as Noah left the shop once more. "I feel badly for how things went when you last came to help me out with that gate."

"It's fine," Thomas said with a sigh. He had no intention of fighting over it. They'd made themselves clear.

"Susan put together some winter clothes for your daughter," Ben said. "She dug them out early. She wanted to make sure Rue had what she needed."

"She needs friends, Ben," Thomas said curtly.

"Yah." Ben nodded a couple of times. "Maybe we can sort something out in that respect, too."

Rue didn't need friends who had been guilted into spending time with her, either. Rue needed real, honest love—like the kind she'd been getting from Mary and Patience.

"I dropped the bag of clothes by your place before I came to town," Ben said. "Rue was very polite and well mannered. I thought you might like to know that."

"*Yah*, that's good to hear," Thomas agreed.

"Your rooster attacked me, though," Ben said with a low laugh. "I thought you were going to eat that bird. He'll be tough as rubber by the time you get him in a pot."

"I can't cook him," Thomas replied. "Rue's attached to him."

"She named him, I think?" Ben asked.

"Toby. That's Toby the rooster." Thomas met the other man's gaze, and for the first time, he realized, he was having banter with another *daet*. It felt good— better than he imagined it would.

"I got overly attached to a turkey when I was a kid," Ben said. "I named it and begged my *daet* not to kill it for Christmas dinner."

"Did he save it?" Thomas asked. Was there an elderly turkey running around their farm because of a small boy's love?

"What? No..." Ben shrugged. "We'd raised that turkey specifically for Christmas dinner. So my *daet* butchered it. It took me a full year to forgive him, though. And by the next Christmas, I still carried a small grudge against him. But we had a family of ten *kinner* to feed, plus the guests who'd come by. That turkey was food, and there was no getting around it."

A family with ten children... That was the kind of

family an Amish man dreamed of. That was the kind of family that would give Rue the siblings who would help her feel her place in this community. They'd belong to each other... Or that was what he'd thought, at least. Thomas looked at his friend thoughtfully for a moment.

"Do you wish he'd saved it?" Thomas asked, at last. "I mean, you know that they had to eat it, and all, but do you wish he'd done it for you?"

Ben's expression softened and he rubbed a hand through his scraggly beard. "It would have meant the world to me if he had."

A family with ten *kinner*, and a boy's heart had still turned to the Christmas turkey. But even with all that family around, a loving gesture for one little boy would have made all the difference for him.

"Look, if you want to sell me the bird, you can tell her that it went to a farm, and I'll cook that rooster myself," Ben said. "If that helps you in getting rid of it."

"No," Thomas said. "Rue has already decided that Toby is part of the family, and I've been informed that we don't eat family. I suppose we shouldn't let neighbors eat family, either. It's the spirit of the thing."

Ben chuckled. "Fair enough. Well, I just wanted to make sure that we were square between us, Thomas."

"*Yah*, we're fine," Thomas replied. "Thanks."

Ben nodded and turned toward the door. Thomas watched him go, then picked up the sandpaper once more. But this time he stared down at it, his mind spinning.

Was it possible to love his daughter so well that she found the roots she needed without brothers and sisters? Maybe he'd been defining family wrong... Sometimes families looked different because of how life had unfolded. He was a single *daet*, and his *mamm* was returning to the community... Maybe Rue needed to see his *mamm* loved well, in spite of the hard times, in spite of her changed views. Maybe Rue needed to see a wife loved deeply, whether or not she could have babies. Maybe the family Rue needed to see wasn't the traditional Amish family of a *mamm*, a *daet* and a large group of siblings. Perhaps his daughter needed to see their family just as it was, complete with imperfections, hurts, hopes and devotion. And maybe, just maybe, Patience could be a part of it...

She didn't want to be the one who held him back from the family she thought he wanted, but there might be a way to convince her that if she agreed to be his, he wasn't settling at all—he was reaching for the highest happiness he could hope for on this earth.

"Noah!" Thomas brushed off his clothes with a sweep of his hands, and headed for the door that led to the sales shop.

An older Amish couple were just leaving, and both Noah and Amos looked up.

"I know this is a lot to ask since I've been taking so much time off for my daughter, but would you mind if I left a couple of hours early today?" Thomas asked.

The clock on the wall showed it was nearly three o'clock, and school would be letting out in a matter of minutes.

"What's the rush?" Amos asked with a frown.

"I'm going to do something that might be incredibly

stupid," Thomas admitted. "But then again, it might be wonderful."

Noah exchanged a look with Amos and both men grinned.

"So you're going to propose, are you?" Amos asked.

Thomas shot them an irritated look. "I'll make up the time. However, this goes, I'll need to be working— either to save for a wedding, or to drown my sorrow."

"Don't let us keep you," Noah said, gesturing toward the door. "And I'm praying for the wedding, Thomas. She's a good choice!"

Thomas headed for the door and refused to look back. He knew that Noah and Amos meant well, but right now he didn't want their good-humored ribbing. What he wanted was to get to the schoolhouse and see Patience... Because that was where his heart already was. He needed to see her once more, hold her hand again, and if she'd accept him, pull her back into his arms for good. He didn't know if she would accept him, but he was adding his prayers to his brother's.

Gott, I believe You've shown me the wife for me...if only You'd bring us together.

Chapter Fourteen

"Bartholomew, you may ring the bell now," Patience said.

If she had to be honest, she'd been looking forward to the sound of that clanging bell overhead, too, and not just because she was tired. The *kinner* were wonderful—three first graders, and four eighth graders, with a spattering of *kinner* in the grades between. They were good kids—smart, eager and funny. She was looking forward to this year together, and it would be better still when she could finally put her heartbreak behind her.

But today, her pain was very, very fresh.

Bartholomew, an eighth-grade boy, opened the door that revealed the bell's cord and gave it a hard pull. The bell clanged above them, and the *kinner* jumped to their feet, chattering away excitedly.

There were a couple of buggies waiting for some smaller *kinner* who had too far to walk, but most of them would walk home, their lunch boxes swinging at their sides and backpacks holding their first homework.

"Goodbye, Teacher," said Naomi, a little girl not much bigger than Rue was. She had similar straight blond hair pulled back into a ponytail and she smiled up at Patience adoringly.

"Goodbye, Naomi," Patience said with a smile. "I'll see you tomorrow."

Naomi dashed out, her older sister and brother already outside the schoolhouse, and Patience tried to soothe the sadness that welled in her heart when she thought of Rue. One day, she'd be Rue's teacher, but it wasn't quite enough. Not for the love she already carried for the girl. To be called Teacher would be an honor, but to be called Mamm...

She pushed back the thought—it wasn't wise to let herself think of such things. She knew better than to allow herself to long for things that couldn't be hers.

"Have a good day, Patience," one of the *mamms* called into the door.

"Thank you! You, too!" Patience called back.

She went down the rows of desks, picking up bits of garbage on the floor and straightening a chair or tucking a paper inside a desk. She stood and looked around. This was her classroom, and it would mean something different to every student she taught, but to her, it would be a refuge—somewhere she could be something more.

The front door opened again just as Patience bent down to pick up a little carved horse. It was Naomi's, and Patience had made her promise to take it home and not bring it back to school again. But she hadn't confiscated it. She wanted to give Naomi the chance to do the right thing.

"Patience?"

She froze at the sound of Thomas's voice, and then looked up, breathless. Thomas stood in the doorway, then the door swung shut behind him, leaving them alone. She held the little horse in the palm of her hand, and she put it down on the top of Naomi's desk.

"Hi..." she said. "I wasn't expecting you."

"I know," Thomas said. He wound his way through the desks toward her, and when he got to her, she felt the tears well up inside her. She'd pushed her heart-break back all day for the sake of the *kinner*, and now facing him...

"This isn't fair, Thomas," she said. "I'm trying to be strong—"

"Patience, let me tell you about something, and then I promise that I'll leave you be. But hear me out."

Patience nodded, sucking in a stabilizing breath.

"I want to marry you," he said.

She shook her head. "But we've been over this—"

"I had a bit of an epiphany today," he said quietly. "It had to do with Toby the rooster and Ben Smoker's turkey, and..."

"This doesn't make any sense," she said, a smile toying at her lips.

"Long story short, my daughter needs love," he said. "She needs real, honest love. She doesn't need a perfect Amish setup, she needs to see her grandmother loved in spite of a difficult history, and she needs to have a ratty rooster that is part of the family just because she loves it. I've been seeing this all wrong, Patience. A family's love isn't purer for the number of *kinner* born to it, and a child doesn't feel more loved because of a wealth of siblings. Love is…love! It's a mother finding a place with her family, even after years of heartbreak. It's two brothers who look up to a man like a father, even though he is no blood relative. It's a man and a woman who love each other so deeply—" he reached out and caught her hand "—that they choose to face whatever Gott brings them side by side, shoulder to shoulder."

"Is that me?" she whispered.

"Yah." He tugged her closer. "I want that to be you. I'm not going to regret anything, Patience. I believe Gott brought us together for a reason. How many women would be able to love my little Englisher girl the way you do? How many would be wary of her influencing the other *kinner*? But you've loved Rue for the little person she is right from the start. I want my daughter to grow up with you as her *mamm*. And I want you as my wife."

"Even with no other *kinner*?" she asked.

"That is in Gott's hands," he replied. "Maybe we'll adopt. Maybe we won't. But Gott started something in us, Patience, and I believe this is something…" he touched her cheek with the back of one finger, the scent of wood shavings close and comforting "…this is something wonderful."

She nodded slowly, and she thought of the Kauffmans with their devoted marriage and their life of loving the ones who needed a *mamm* and *daet*, even for a little while. A life together, finding a way to love those around them, raising one little girl with love and purpose and direction…

"Patience, I love you," he added pleadingly.

"I love you, too." She lifted her gaze to meet his.

"Enough to marry me?" he asked hopefully. "Enough to trust me to never look back, never look to the side… Enough to be ours?"

"Yah."

Thomas slipped his arms around her and lowered his lips over hers. He pulled her in close, his stubble tickling her chin as he kissed her. His arms were strong and she let herself melt into his embrace.

The door opened just then, and Patience startled. She pulled back, instinctively putting her hand up to her *kapp* to make sure her hair was in place.

"Teacher?" Naomi said uncertainly.

"Naomi!" Patience laughed breathily, tugging herself out of Thomas's arms. She went to her desk and picked up the toy horse. "You forgot this, didn't you?"

"Yah…" Naomi looked over at Thomas uncertainly, and Patience brought her the toy.

"You run along home now," Patience said. "And no more bringing toys to school, okay?"

"Okay." Naomi headed back out, and Patience nearly wilted when the door closed once more.

"You said yes, right?" Thomas said. "You'd just agreed to be my wife?"

"I said yes," she confirmed, and a smile spread over her face.

Thomas crossed the distance between them and kissed her once more. "I'll talk to the bishop today, then, because I have a feeling the rumors are about to explode around here—starting at that little girl's house. He'd better be in the know."

Patience couldn't help but laugh. "I think you're right."

And this time when Patience looked around the schoolroom, she saw more than a chance at a life where she could contribute, she saw a future with a husband by her side and a little girl who'd call her Mamm. A family of her own—maybe not the most traditional in appearance, but purposefully pieced together by Gott's own hands.

And when Gott brought a family together, let no man put it asunder.

Epilogue

The wedding was held in late October after all the harvesting was done and the community was free to celebrate. Patience's family came for the wedding, and the community of Redemption pulled together to cook and prepare for the only wedding that fall.

Thomas rented a house on another Amish family's property. It was a little house originally meant for some farm employees to live in, but it was just perfect for their little family—three bedrooms, a large kitchen, a small sitting room and a bathroom. That was all—but what else did they need? Patience had already set up the kitchen the way she wanted it to be arranged, and Thomas had carefully built their new bedroom set—polishing it by hand. He'd made a special little bed for Rue, too—she'd need more than just the cot she'd been sleeping on so far.

But this wedding wasn't only about him and Patience, it was about Rue, too. This wedding was going to join Thomas and Patience as husband and wife, and

Rue would get a *mamm* of her very own. And for this happy day, Thomas's handiwork wasn't what would matter most to his little girl.

So that morning, while the women put the last of the food into the refrigerated trailer, and while Patience got ready for the wedding in Mammi's bedroom with the help of her mother and two of her sisters, Thomas sat with his daughter in the bedroom that used to be his. He was already dressed in his Sunday best, and Rue was wearing a pink dress just like the other women who were standing as Patience's *newehockers* for the day.

"It's a wedding quilt," Thomas said as Rue unfolded the quilt that Patience had sewn late into the evenings, stitching together squares of Rue's clothing from the suitcase. "But it's a special one. Patience said it was more important that you have your quilt than we have a new one for our bed."

Besides, his mother and Mary had been staying up late into the evenings, too, sewing some quilts to be used on their beds during that winter. Each stitch was sewn with love.

"That's my unicorn shirt," Rue whispered, running her fingers over the familiar fabric. "And that's my striped dress—and my pink shorts!"

Thomas ran his hand over Rue's pale hair.

"Do you like it, Rue?" he asked.

"*Yah.* It's my favorite," she said, and she hugged the quilt against her chest. "And today is a happy day. It's the day you and Patience become a mister and missus."

"Well, we Amish don't use those titles, Rue," he said.

Rue put her small hand on his knee and gave him

a serious look. "It's an important day, the day you become a mister, Daddy."

Thomas laughed and scooped her off the bed and into his arms.

"I'll explain all of that to you later. But right now, I want you to go into the bedroom where Patience is getting ready, because she's going to need you."

"And what will you do?" Rue asked.

"I'm going out to the tent. I have to wait there until you and Patience come. It's what the men do when they're getting married."

Thomas carried Rue out into the hallway, and he put her down in front of Mary's bedroom door just as his *mamm* came up the stairs. There were female voices coming from inside and a peal of laughter.

"Oh, no, you don't!" Rachel said with a laugh. "The bride is to be left alone until the ceremony. You know that, son."

Thomas bent down and kissed his *mamm*'s cheek. "I'll leave Rue with you, then."

He shot his mother a grin as she paused with her hand on the doorknob to Mary's bedroom, refusing to open it even a crack until he headed down the stairs. And Rue stood there, standing tall and proud with a smile on her face.

"He's gonna be a mister," Rue told her grandmother seriously. "And I think then I'd better call him Daet."

Thomas pretended not to hear, but he smothered a laugh. Was that the line for Rue when she'd finally let him be her Amish *daet* instead of a daddy—the day he married Patience? To finally be called Daet by his little girl would be the finest wedding gift anyone could offer him, and he sent up a prayer of wordless thanks to Gott for all of these blessings.

Patience was up there getting dressed, hearing all the last-minute advice from her married sisters and from her *mamm*. And they'd need all of it—all the advice and love and support that their families and their community could offer them.

As for Thomas, Amos and Noah didn't have much advice for him between them except to say, "Remember how blessed you are in marrying that woman. And treat her like you're grateful. We think that should cover it."

It likely would. And he was grateful. Thomas paused in the kitchen and looked up the stairs. He couldn't wait to say his vows and to finally claim Patience as his own.

"Out, out, out!" Mary said, flapping a towel at him. "Everyone is ready for you in the tent—they sent one of the *kinner* to tell me. Let's get you wed, Thomas. It's high time."

Thomas headed out the door to where Amos and Noah waited for him under trees ablaze in golden splendor. The men rubbed their hands together in the chilly autumn air, their breath hanging in front of them as they hunched their shoulders up against the chill. It was colder than usual, and while there wasn't snow yet, there would be soon. Noah grinned at him and Amos just stood there with a goofy smile on his face.

"Let's go," Thomas said. "I'm getting married today."

Then the three of them headed for the tent, the golden leaves swirling free in a gust of wind. Today was his wedding day, and in the presence of his family and community, he'd vow to love Patience, to stand by her, to defend her and to honor her.

At last, Rue would have a *mamm*, and his heart would be filled right to the brim.

Gott was good.

* * * * *

Dear Reader,

The idea for this book started with a child's tantrum. All kids kick up a fit at some point, no matter how well they're raised or how earnest their parents are. So what happens when a really stubborn little girl is introduced to the Amish family she's never known? And who would be more panicked—the little girl, or the brand-new dad?

I hope you enjoy this story of new beginnings and a little girl's fragile heart. And I hope you'll take a look at my backlist of other published books at PatriciaJohns-Romance.com. You can also find me on Facebook and Twitter, where I enjoy connecting with my readers.

Much love from my home to yours,
Patricia

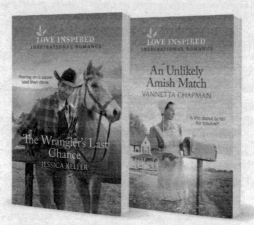

COMING NEXT MONTH FROM
Love Inspired

Available June 16, 2020

AN AMISH MOTHER'S SECRET PAST
Green Mountain Blessings • by Jo Ann Brown
Widow Rachel Yoder has a secret: she's a military veteran trying to give her children a new life among the Amish. Though she's drawn to bachelor Isaac Kauffman, she knows she can't tell him the truth—or give him her heart. Because Rachel can never be the perfect Plain wife he's looking for...

THE BLACK SHEEP'S SALVATION
by Deb Kastner
A fresh start for Logan Maddox and his son, who has autism, means returning home and getting Judah into the educational program that best serves his needs. The problem? Molly Winslow—the woman he left behind years ago—is the teacher. Might little Judah reunite Logan and Molly for good?

HOME TO HEAL
The Calhoun Cowboys • by Lois Richer
After doctor Zac Calhoun is blinded during an incident on his mission trip, he needs help recuperating...and hiring nurse Abby Armstrong is the best option. But as she falls for the widower and his little twin girls, can she find a way to heal their hearts, as well?

A FATHER'S PROMISE
Bliss, Texas • by Mindy Obenhaus
Stunned to discover he has a child, Wes Bishop isn't sure he's father material. But his adorable daughter needs him, and he can't help feeling drawn to her mother—a woman he's finally getting to know. Can this sudden dad make a promise of forever?

THE COWBOY'S MISSING MEMORY
Hill Country Cowboys • by Shannon Taylor Vannatter
After waking up with a brain injury caused by a bull-riding accident, Clint Rawlins can't remember the past two years. His occupational therapist, Lexie Parker, is determined to help him recover his short-term memory. But keeping their relationship strictly professional may be harder than expected.

HIS DAUGHTER'S PRAYER
by Danielle Thorne
Struggling to keep his antiques store open, single dad Mark Chatham can't turn down his high school sweetheart, Callie Hargrove, when she moves back to town and offers her assistance in the shop. But as she works to save his business, can Callie avoid losing her heart to his little girl...and to Mark?

LOOK FOR THESE AND OTHER LOVE INSPIRED BOOKS WHEREVER BOOKS ARE SOLD, INCLUDING MOST BOOKSTORES, SUPERMARKETS, DISCOUNT STORES AND DRUGSTORES.

LICNM0620

"Isaac is in the barn. Sarah, you should go say hello."

"Are you sure?" Sarah bit her lower lip and began walking toward the barn. Her pulse raced as butterflies filled her stomach. What would Isaac think of her? Would he be happy to see her again? What should she say? She stepped through the open doorway and paused to let her eyes adjust to the darkness. She spotted him a few feet away. He was on one knee tightening a screw in a stall door. His hat was pushed back on his head. She couldn't see his face. He hadn't heard her come in.

Suddenly she was a giddy sixteen-year-old again about to burst out laughing for the sheer joy of it. She quietly tiptoed up behind him and cupped her hands over his eyes. "Guess who?" she whispered in his ear.

"I have no idea."

The voice wasn't right. Strong hands gripped her wrists and pulled her hands away. His hat fell off as he turned his head to stare up at her. She saw a riot of dark brown curls, not straw-blond hair. She didn't know this man.

A scowl drew his brows together. "I still don't know who you are."

She pulled her hands free and stumbled backward as embarrassment robbed her of speech. The man retrieved his hat and rose to his feet. "I assume you were expecting someone else?"

"I'm sorry," she managed to squeak.

The man in front of her settled his hat on his head. He wasn't as tall as Isaac, but he was a head taller than Sarah. He had rugged good looks, dark eyes and a full mouth, which was turned up at one corner as if a grin was about to break free. "I take it you know my brother Isaac."

He was laughing at her.

The dark-haired stranger folded his arms over his chest. "I'm Levi Raber."

Of course, he would be the annoying older brother. So much for making a good first impression on Isaac's family.

Don't miss
The Promise *by Patricia Davids,*
available now wherever
HQN Books and ebooks are sold.

HQNBooks.com

PHPDEXP0620TP